THE I

The young man turned
I was thankful that I w
so that he couldn't se
press my hands agair

Because the man
charmingly enquiring half-smile was not about to a
cousinly cry of recognition.

He was not Tony Maynard. I had never seen him before in my life.

Estelle Thompson has written many novels, a number of which have been translated into several languages, serialised in women's magazines and broadcast on radio. She lives in Australia where she particularly enjoys badminton and listening to music.

ESTELLE THOMPSON

THE HEIR TO FAIRFIELD

Woman's Weekly Fiction

A Woman's Weekly Paperback
THE HEIR TO FAIRFIELD

First published in Great Britain 1983
by Robert Hale Ltd
This edition published 1995
by Mandarin Paperbacks
an imprint of Reed Consumer Books Ltd
Michelin House, 81 Fulham Road, London SW3 6RB
and Auckland, Melbourne, Singapore and Toronto

A CIP catalogue record for this title
is available from the British Library
ISBN 186056 070 9

Printed and bound in Great Britain
by Cox & Wyman Ltd, Reading, Berkshire

One

The daffodils in St David's Park as I passed said it was spring, but an icy wind was blowing and Mt Wellington had a cloak of snow across its shoulders where it stood protectively behind the city.

The snow and the cold were hardly to be compared with the winters of Yorkshire I had grown up with, but after the relative mildness of the Sydney winter I had just experienced I felt this pale blue Tasmanian morning sharply chilled, but with a clear-cut beauty that made me whistle happily to myself as I turned my very second-hand Datsun southward through Hobart's morning traffic.

I stopped the car for a few minutes beside the old Shot Tower where once gun-shot had been made, and reflected that in Tasmania far more than anywhere else in the country one was constantly reminded of Australia's grim beginnings as a massive dumping-ground for British convicts. It was one of the things which this island State found fascinating to tourists.

But I wasn't here as a tourist. Not exactly.

Somewhere not far from here, according to the road-map, was a villlage called Fallow and – perhaps only because of the odd name – I carried a memory from my childhood that this was where my grandmother Maynard, my mother's mother, lived. If in fact she was still alive.

I wasn't really sure what had prompted my visit to the old lady I had never seen and knew virtually nothing about. Probably due to a fragmented family life, I had never had a strong sense of family ties. My mother had married Englishman Tom Beaconsfield and had gone with him from Tasmania to the Yorkshire town where his dental practice was and where I was born a couple of years later, destined to be their only child. My childhood was happily normal until my mother died when I was fourteen and my father, distractedly lonely, remarried within a year. His second wife and I were neither friends nor enemies. I left home at eighteen and trained as a teacher, and when my father died suddenly my stepmother and I drifted farther apart and eventually simply lost touch. I think my father had corresponded occasionally with my grandmother Maynard after my mother's death, but to me she was no more than a name. I knew I had heard that my grandfather had died but I had little idea how long ago.

I checked the map again. Fallow was only a few kilometres away. As I slid back into the car I reflected it was probable my grandmother had died, or had moved from the orchard which had been her home all her married life. Lack of family had never troubled me. I'd gone from home young, and had had good friends in England. I supposed it was only a sudden sense of being so far from home that had triggered the burst of sentiment which had brought me to look for someone who was "family".

If I hadn't seen the name on the roadside sign I mightn't have realized it was a village at all, but I smiled with instinctive pleasure as I stopped the car beside the weather-board building which doubled as post office and general store and, apart from a tiny service-station with one yellow petrol pump, was Fallow's sole business-house. I love tiny villages, and this one, with a cluster of elms behind the post office and the still-bare-limbed willows leaning reflectively over a little stream, was almost like a breath of England – which no doubt, I thought, annoyed some stout-hearted Australians, but which delighted me.

I pulled my suede car-coat closely around me as I went up the four wooden steps into the post office. Her Majesty's postal services occupied one end of a longish varnished wooden counter, most of the rest of which was taken up with groceries. The postmistress-cum-storekeeper, a thin, wiry little woman, looked me over swiftly, clearly aware I was a stranger.

"Can I help you at all?"

"I'm looking for a Mrs Maynard – Mrs Margaret Maynard," I told her.

The woman's face at once lit with interest. "Oh, old Mrs Maynard of Fairfield orchard? You're looking for work there, I suppose?"

I hesitated, unsure why I didn't simply say: 'She's my grandmother' – except that, pleasant as this sharp-eyed little woman was, she struck me as being an incorrigible gossip and my instinctive reaction was to draw back into my shell. So I said cautiously that I might be interested in a job.

The postmistress nodded. "Yes, I thought you must be after the job as companion to the old lady, her needing a new one now."

"Is she ill?" I asked.

"Heart," the postmistress said solemnly. "Very bad, I believe. She's had several real nasty turns. They say the least tiny shock could kill her. It's a marvel the last awful business didn't, and that's a fact. Really, you'd be wanted more as a housekeeper, no nursing or anything like that. Mrs Maynard isn't an invalid in the strict sense of the word – she can still get about a bit and all that. Sharp as a tack in her mind, you know – marvellous old lady."

There was genuine affection and admiration in the tone. I wondered briefly what the 'awful business' was. "How does she manage to run an orchard if she's so ill?" I asked.

"Ah, it was an absolute godsend, her grandson coming when he did. Made all the difference in the world, that did. Such a fine young man – and so competent he's become, especially seeing he didn't know an apple from a pear, hardly, when he came."

"Her grandson?" I asked sharply.

She nodded. "Mr Tony Maynard. Oh, twenty-seven, twenty-eight, I'd say he'd be. Came out from England two years ago to visit, and stayed. Wonderful for Mrs Maynard.

She thinks the world of him, and well she might. Oh, she's a fine businesswoman, no question of that, the way she's run that orchard all these years since her husband died. But the way her health is now, she'd never cope without young Mr Maynard. She's just too frail. And Harry Gootch – he's the orchard foreman – well, Harry's a good solid worker and he *knows all the practical* side of orchard work, no doubt of that, but he couldn't have taken over the management; and young Mr Maynard seems very able that way, and of course the old lady would *trust* him the way she'd never be able to trust an outsider."

She chattered on happily, but I was scarcely listening.

Tony – my cousin Tony – here? And running the orchard? Somehow, that just didn't fit the Tony I remembered. But then, how long was it since I'd seen him, or even heard of him, for that matter? Almost ten years, I supposed. People change.

Apart from my grandmother, Tony Maynard was my only surviving relative – my mother's brother's son. His parents, like mine, had gone to England when Tony was two years old and, like me, he was their only child. My uncle had been a doctor – a surgeon in a London clinic. He and my aunt were killed in a place crash while returning from a holiday in Austria when Tony was fifteen. I had seen Tony from time to time until his parents' death, when he went to live with friends of theirs, but I had seen him only once since, when he was about eighteen. His parents had left him little money, having been people who lived for the moment, and Tony, who had taken an apprenticeship as a motor mechanic, seemed cast in a similar mould.

Tony liked the lively life. But that had been Tony the boy of eighteen.

"So," I said to the postmistress with an amused smile, "if I want the job as Mrs Maynard's housekeeper, it's to Mr Tony Maynard I should apply?"

She nodded briskly. "That or any other job on the orchard, dearie." Her eyes went to the window. "Why, there's a stroke of luck for you – that's Mr Maynard stopping in the Landrover now. Now I won't have to give you directions on how to get to Fairfield. My Bill says the surest way for anyone to get lost is to ask me for directions."

I turned, smiling, to face the door, waiting for Tony to come in, wondering if he'd recognize me. After all, I'd been only a schoolgirl of fifteen last time we'd met.

Heavy boots bounded crisply up the steps and a tall, broad-shouldered young man with short, wavy fair hair, blue eyes and devastatingly good looks strode in with a cheerful grin. He had a determined chin and a toughly muscular look which suggested he would be a good man to have on your side in a brawl.

"Morning, Mrs Bishop. A packet of weed for the machine, please." He held up his pipe. "And would you believe we're out of sugar and coffee. Coffee! Such a catastrophe can't be endured."

His tone was joking, but there was a hint of exasperation under the lightness. "Things like that never happened when we were in Janet's capable hands."

"Mater of fact, Mr Maynard," the postmistress told him as she put tobacco, coffee and sugar on the counter, "this young lady is enquiring about the advertisement for the position of housekeeper."

At that moment nothing was farther from my mind than to protest that this was only Mrs Bishop's interpretation of my enquiry.

The young man turned his head and saw me for the first time. I was thankful that I was standing with my back to the window so that he couldn't see my face too clearly, or notice I had to press my hands against the counter behind me for support.

Because the man who stood looking at me with a charmingly enquiring half-smile was not about to utter a cousinly cry of recognition.

He was not Tony Maynard. I had never seen him before in my life.

Two

I was never sure, afterwards, why I didn't simply blurt out that this man was an imposter. Perhaps I was just rendered numb and speechless with shock.

Or perhaps it was the postmistress' remark on the state of my grandmother's health – "least tiny shock could kill her." And, I thought with a flare of anger, she's *my* grandmother, not his, whatever game he's playing.

The two of us had looked at each other appraisingly for what seemed an age but in reality was probably about three seconds. There was a degree of admiration in the man's glance – the kind of frank admiration with which, I felt, he would look at any presentable female. "That sounds promising. I'm Tony Maynard, Miss? –"

I hesitated a fraction of a second, suddenly filled with a sharp awareness that here, in this queer farcical situation, something was very wrong, perhaps dangerously wrong. It might be better if no-one knew my identity, at least until I had time to think. I cast hastily around in my mind for a new surname, and my glance rested on a rack of bread. "Baker," I said. "Anne Baker," and the tiny pause went unnoticed.

"Well," the man who called himself Tony Maynard said pleasantly, "suppose you follow me out to the orchard – that's your car outside? It's only a kilometre or so, and we can discuss the situation."

I managed to say that sounded like a good idea, and he paid for his purchases, scooped them up and stood aside to let me go out first.

I followed the Landrover like an automaton, blind to the countryside, my mind feeling as if I were coming out of a drugged sleep. What was this man playing at? Why had he come, posing as an old lady's grandson?

The answer to that seemed obvious enough: fraud. Precisely what kind of fraud was hard to say. But whatever his reasons were, what he was doing was surely criminal. Then, I told myself, the sensible thing was to go at once to the police. All I had to do was to let the Landrover get out of sight around the next bend, stop, turn my own car around, and go back the way I had come. Even when the man realized I had gone, he couldn't know I was any kind of threat to him, and would shrug me off as eccentric.

But I couldn't forget that Mrs Bishop had said my grandmother's health was so precarious that any shock could kill her. That might have been an overdramatization of the facts by a gossipy woman, or it might have been plain truth. And certainly it would be no small shock for an old lady to be told that the young man she had accepted and loved and trusted for two years was a fraud and a criminal.

At least until I knew the truth about Margaret Maynard's health I must hold my tongue.

I needed time – time to assess the situation, time to think what to do. Perhaps if I could get the position of housekeeper-companion, it would at least give me the time I needed to think.

At the moment there was only one thing I could be sure of: although Margaret Maynard was a complete stranger to me, someone I hadn't even thought much about, she was my grandmother and I couldn't just turn my back on the situation and walk away, saying it was none of my business.

I had been so intent on my own thoughts and on mechanically following the Landrover that it was only when the man calling himself Tony turned off on to a gravelled road, drove a short way between rows of apple trees and stopped before a long, low-set house, that I took any notice of my surroundings.

I stopped my car beside the Landrover and stepped out with an involuntary little exclamation of pleasure.

The house was colonial, of sandstone blocks with a

terracotta tiled roof and a flagstoned verandah along its full length. It was set in green lawns which ran back to elms and a huge old oak which some early settler homesick for England must have planted at least a century before, and a couple of dark green conifers. Clusters of azaleas and rhododendrons would be a mass of loveliness in a few weeks.

But, charming as the house was, it was the view it commanded which really caught my delighted attention, and for the moment I forgot this queer situation I had blundered into. Only the most insensitive of human beings could have failed to be enchanted. The house overlooked a wide expanse of orchard and farmland which swept down in a gentle slope toward the D'Entrecastaux Channel, blue in the sunlight, and the hump of an island beyond.

"It does have that effect on people," the man's voice said quietly beside me.

I started and turned, to find him watching me with a little smile that was not in the least unpleasant, and I was jerked back from the loveliness of the scene to the ugliness of the situation.

"It's very beautiful," I said simply. "I was so intent on following the Landrover I hadn't noticed the scenery until we stopped."

He nodded. "Well, come in, Miss Baker. There's an excellent view from the loungeroom windows, and it's much warmer.

I think my grandmother's still in her room, but of course you'll want to meet her if you seriously consider taking on the job."

As he spoke he ushered me into a large and pleasant room where a small log fire burned cheerfully in the grate and deep green curtains were drawn back from wide windows which had a splendid view. A black and white cat curled in an easy chair near the fire lifted its head and eyed me curiously, decided I represented no threat to its comfort, stretched one front leg and went back to sleep.

"Make yourself comfortable," the man said. "I'll take these things out to the kitchen. Mrs Gootch is still there, so she'll make us some coffee."

He went out and I looked around almost unseeingly. I had an impression of books and comfortable chairs and a general much-lived-in atmosphere in the room. I walked over to the chair where the cat slept and began stroking under its upturned chin while it stretched and purred ecstatically, but it was an unthinking gesture on my part, motivated purely by my natural instincts which always make me gravitate towards animals. My mind was racing.

If I was going to attempt this masquerade – and I could see no alternative – there were three things I had better adjust to, and quickly. I had to make myself accept that for all practical purposes this man's name was Tony Maynard and I must think of him as that. Second, I had to unfailingly call my grandmother Mrs Maynard; that would be easier, since she was a stranger. And third, I was Anne Baker and I must learn to answer to that and to remember that Anne Baker knew no more of the Maynard family than she was told by the people in this household.

Tony came back with a tray holding two stoneware mugs of coffee, milk, sugar and a plate of homemade biscuits, which he set down on a low table. Basically there was a resemblance between him and my cousin: the wavy fair hair, blue eyes, the height and build. This man could have been Tony's brother, had he had one.

"Push the cat out of there if you want the chair by the fire," he said a shade impatiently.

I shook my head. "I was just making friends." I walked over and sat by the table.

The coffee was welcome and Tony made easy small talk. Then he put down his empty cup and leaned back and looked at me.

"Why do you want this job?" he asked bluntly.

"Because unfortunately I haven't yet amassed a sufficiently large fortune to allow me to retire in luxury on a tropical island," I answered drily.

He made an impatient gesture. "Miss Baker, you're an intelligent woman and I imagine an educated one. Why choose a housekeeping job?"

I hesitated. "I'm a teacher by profession. I taught in England for five years, and when I came to Australia in February I took a temporary teaching position in Sydney. Then I began to feel I wasn't going to see anything of a new country by staying in a Sydney classroom, so I bought myself a secondhand car and drove to Melbourne, took the ferry to Devonport, and then drove down the east coast to Hobart. I like what I've seen of Tasmania and I'd like to stay a while. This job seemed to offer something different. I don't see any particular merit in simply sticking to one job all my life."

He nodded. "Fair enough. But if you take this job, you'll understand, I'm sure, that my grandmother would want you to regard it as a long-term thing – something that you'd be prepared to stick to for, say, a year. It would be difficult for her to adjust to a succession of new people."

"I can understand that. Certainly as far as I'm concerned I'd be willing to accept the position on a long-term basis – barring unforseen circumstances, of course."

He shot me an odd look, but only said conversationally, "Why did you come to Australia?"

I shrugged. "A love affair went wrong and I just decided to cut my losses and make a clean new start – if one ever can. At least going to a new country offers that kind of illusion."

I paused a moment. "Anyway, I had no family ties to hold me back. And it was winter and Australia sounded warm," I added lightly.

He raised one sardonic eyebrow. "Sydney in February should have fulfilled your expectations."

"A little too well," I agreed. "So I headed south before another summer came up. I haven't any qualifications for caring for elderly invalids, I'm afraid, but I come equipped with a reasonable amount of commonsense, I've kept house for myself since I was eighteen, and I'm not particularly afraid of work."

The truth, the whole truth, and nothing but the truth.

The phrase jumped suddenly into my mind. Well, it had seemed sensible to stick to facts; that way, I didn't have to keep remembering what I'd said. I'd told him the truth, and nothing but the truth, I just hadn't told him the whole truth.

"Well," he was saying, "that sounds reasonable to me. My grandmother doesn't need nursing care as such. She can get about, dress herself and all that sort of thing, but she becomes exhausted very easily. What she really needs is an understanding person to be company for her when she wants it, take her meals on the days when she doesn't feel well enough to come out of her room, drive her to town or to visit her friends when she feels like it – all that sort of thing. She shouldn't be left alone for more than short periods, because of the fact she is in constant danger of a heart attack, though it's not always a bad one, and she has pills to put under her tongue if an attack occurs. But most of all she needs someone to simply completely take charge of the house and garden. Mrs Gootch is helping out at the moment, but she's the wife of the orchard foreman – they have a cottage on the orchard – and she has her own house and family to attend to."

I nodded. "I think I could cope – providing Mrs Maynard likes me."

"And providing you like her," he said. "She looks incredibly frail and her heart is very weak, but her mind isn't, and neither is her will, and she has a habit of saying what she thinks."

He stood up. "Well, come along and meet her."

He showed me along a hall and tapped on a polished timber door that I thought vaguely was probably cedar. I hoped no-one could guess my knees had suddenly begun to tremble violently as the sheer enormity of what I was doing hit me. The woman I was about to meet was not just a prospective employer, however much I might try to condition myself to think of her in that role.

She was my grandmother, my blood tied to hers, and nothing could change that.

The voice which said, "Come in," was clear and light in tone, but confident and pleasant.

"Grandma," Tony was saying as he opened the door, "This is Miss Baker – Anne Baker. She's come about the housekeeping job."

The old lady in the easy chair by the window put down the book she was reading and looked at me. Her wavy white hair was cut fairly short and cut well, so that it framed and softened the intelligent face. Her hands were painfully thin and the skin had the transparent look of age. Margaret Maynard must have been a beautiful woman when she was younger. There was about her one thing which did not fade with time: a grace, quite unstudied, of posture and movement, combined with an air of self-assurance which had about it a hint of arrogance.

She sat quite still, simply looking at me with the sureness of someone who was perfectly at ease, perfectly sure of herself, with no sense of being obliged to please the world around her; but when she smiled the keen blue eyes lit with warmth and I found myself smiling back and for a moment it was as if she knew my secret and it was a bond, something shared between us.

"How do you do, Mrs Maynard," I said quietly.

"Sit down, my dear," she said with a gesture to the other chair which was drawn around to half-face hers. "Tony, have you thought to offer Miss Baker coffee or something? It's such a chilly day."

"Yes, Grandma, I've played the perfect host. Now I'll leave you girls to talk. I'll be in the office." He smiled at her and she watched him go with affection in her eyes, and I felt a swift blaze of anger against him.

"Oh, mind Percy, dear," Margaret Maynard said

quickly, at the same moment I noticed that the shadow in the depths of the other armchair was a black cat.

I ran a hand over his back and he responded with a vast yawn. "I say, old chap," I said, "D'you mind? You can have my lap if you like."

He allowed himself to be picked up and set on my knees, where he looked up at me interestedly and a shade warily for a moment, then flopped down contentedly in my lap, sighed and went back to sleep.

I looked up to find Mrs Maynard watching me alertly. "I like animals," I told her.

"Yes," she said. "It's the one thing people can't ever successfully pretend. Now, suppose you tell me something about yourself. You're English, aren't you?"

As we talked I watched her intently. There was no family resemblance that I could see, and certainly she and I were not alike, except that she once must have been about my build. I wondered whether she would see any likeness between me and some member of the family, but I consoled myself with the thought that she would put it down to coincidence.

I told her the things I had told Tony.

"You see, Mrs Maynard, I haven't any nursing qualifications. But I'm willing to try."

"I don't need a nurse," she said crisply. "Janet was a nurse, certainly, but she was looking for change, and she proved a very competent housekeeper. I believe you'd suit me very well, Anne. But you mustn't decide whether or not to take the job until you've seen over the house and the garden, and discussed wages with my grandson."

"How many people are in the household?" I asked.

"Normally, only Tony and myself. But sometimes at weekends and always in school holidays, Drew Thomas comes to stay." She smiled, and I guessed Drew Thomas, whoever he was, had a special place in her affections.

"Drew is the grandson of very old friends of my husband's and mine," she added in explanation. "He's in his final year at High School in Hobart, and the orchard makes a welcome break from study and town life. Now go along and tell Tony to show you over the house, especially the room which would be yours. Go through to the lounge-room and the office is the first door on your left."

As I stood up, carefully transferring Percy back to the comfort of the chair, Mrs Maynard said gravely, "I think it rather courageous of you to be ready to take up this position when the tragedy of poor Janet's not yet finalized. Not, of course, that it could have any possible bearing on you."

I went to find Tony, puzzled. The postmistress had referred to some 'awful business' which must have given Mrs Maynard such a shock that – in her opinion – it could have triggered a heart attack, even a fatal one. Now Mrs Maynard herself had spoken of tragedy involving Janet, her last housekeeper.

Tony showed me over the house, which was large and gracious, with just enough modernization for comfort without being intrusive. The room which would be mine was sunny and bright and attractively furnished. We went out and looked around the garden.

"Soon," Tony commented, "it will be rather lovely when the spring blossoms are out. It's mostly lawn and shrubs, as you can see, plus the rock garden on the slope in front. If you want to amuse yourself by planting other things, that's fine." He gestured sweepingly. "Really, what we'd want you to do is more or less treat the place as if it were yours. Oh, I forgot to mention that besides any casual trips into town Grandma may care to take – and those are very few – you will be needed to drive her into Hobart every fortnight to visit her doctor. If she's ill, he will come out here if called. His number is taped to the wall beside the phone. In the fruit-picking season," he added, "there'll be people everywhere, but they're accommodated in cabins on the orchard and cook and launder for themselves, so there's only my grandmother and myself."

"And Drew Thomas occasionally, I believe," I said.

"Mrs Maynard seems very fond of him."

Tony flicked at a pebble with the toe of his boot. "Yes," he said shortly. "She is."

I wondered why he didn't like Drew Thomas.

"Well," he said, looking at me, "what do you say? Are you willing to take the job on?"

"I'd like to," I said.

I didn't tell him that it would be a very strange job I wouldn't take, in order to have a chance to stay around to see what he was up to.

"Good," he said, looking as if he meant it. "I'll bring your things in from the car."

He carried my suitcases into my room, and as he was about to leave I said:

"I don't want to pry into other people's affairs, but Mrs Maynard spoke of Janet, your last housekeeper, and some tragedy connected with her. She seemed to think I'd know all about it. Should I?"

He looked at me with a curious expression.

"Oh." He hesitated. "I rather took it for granted that you knew, too. But of course that's silly, when you've just come down from Sydney. Yes, I think you should know before you finally decide to stay, though the only possible way you could be involved is psychologically."

He turned away to look out of the window. "Yes, Janet Chisholm was my grandmother's previous companion-housekeeper. A month ago she was murdered."

Three

Murdered.

The word lay like a storm-shadow over the garden in defiance of the clear pale sunlight, and involuntarily I shivered and turned away from the window.

"Come into the lounge by the fire," Tony said. "You've a right to know as much as we know about it," he added as we sat down. "Cigarette?" He proffered the box on the table but I shook my head. "Though actually we know very little."

He lit his pipe, seeming absorbed in the operation as pipe-smokers do. "Janet Chisholm was our housekeeper for over two years – she was here when I arrived. She seemed fond of Grandma and very much a part of the household. She was in her middle thirties, quiet, efficient, pleasant."

"Not the sort of person to have an enemy in the world," I murmured. "That's what the newspapers always say, isn't it?"

"Yes. Well, just about four weeks ago she drove off in her car one evening, saying she was going to visit friends. She didn't come back."

He blew a contemplative cloud of smoke. "We didn't realize at first, next morning, that she was missing. No one heard her car come back, but that didn't mean a thing because she kept her car in the double garage which is separate from the house and of course she had her own house-keys. Drew Thomas was staying here at the time – it was a weekend, a Saturday night – and he and I got up at about the same time, made ourselves coffee in the kitchen and I went out to do a maintenace job on the tractor before breakfast, which is usually about eight o'clock. It wasn't until I came in for breakfast that I learned Janet hadn't come home. She usually took my grandmother a cup of tea about seven or seven-thirty and Grandma wondered why there was no tea and got up to make some for herself, as she was feeling well, and Drew had come in – he'd been for a walk – and he went along and knocked on Janet's door. She didn't answer so he went in and found her bed hadn't been slept in. I went out and checked and her car wasn't back.

"I was hardly back in the house when the police arrived. A truck driver had found Janet an hour or so before, not a quarter of a mile from here. Her car was pulled off to the side of the road and she was lying beside it. The car had a flat tyre – nail in it, they found – and she'd apparently pulled off the road and got out to have a look at the trouble."

He paused. "Someone crushed her skull with the proverbial blunt instrument, and we are left with an unsolved murder. The police swarmed over the place like ants for a week or so and put the entire neighbourhood through the hoop. They still come around occasionally, asking more questions – or the same questions over again to see if they get the same answers."

He grinned crookedly. "That's one advantage of telling the truth: it's easy to keep giving the same answers."

I looked at him. "I'm glad," I said drily, "that you have such a high regard for the truth."

He laughed. "But you will note that my regard for the truth is purely practical."

He was instantly serious again. "Well, a young woman was murdered virtually on our doorstep. Aren't you going to ask any questions?"

"Oh, yes," I told him. "I'm going to ask a great many, when I can think where to begin. For starters, do the police appear to have a suspect?"

There was a slight hesitation before he answered. "Not really."

"Do *you* have a suspect?"

"I haven't any reason to have one. Of course everyone in the district has played detective, I suppose. Without coming up with any answers, I imagine, even to please themselves."

"Was there an obvious motive – sex, robbery?"

"Well, there was no sex attack. Her handbag had been emptied of money, so maybe it was robbery, though I imagine Janet would have been carrying very little money."

"So her handbag could have been emptied to make it look like robbery?"

"That could be, yes. We simply don't know."

I frowned. "It seems a bit too much of a coincidence that someone bent on robbery with violence should happen to be lurking in the exact spot where Janet's car got a flat tyre. And if it was robbery, why didn't the thief take the car as well?"

He shrugged. "It would have been a bit of a risk, to stop and change a tyre with a dead body lying on the grass beside you. Besides, the killer could have had his own car, and just been passing when he saw Janet and saw a chance for easy pickings."

"There were no tyre tracks, no unaccounted footmarks?"

"The police haven't exactly taken us into their confidence, but the verge there is thickly grassed, so I shouldn't think any identifiable marks would be likely."

"You said," I said slowly, "that Janet said she was going to visit friends. Did she say who they were?"

"No. I don't mean by that," he added, "that she was seeming to be secretive. She just said quite casually that she was going to spend the evening with friends."

"Was she going out or coming home when it happened?"

"Going out, apparently, judging by the way the car was facing."

"So she never arrived. Didn't the people she was going to visit phone to find out why she hadn't come?"

He shook his head. "No. Of course, it probably wasn't an arranged visit; she was probably just going to drop in on whoever it was quite casually and unannounced. At any rate the police never found anyone who knew she was going to visit them. Or at least they never found anyone willing to admit she was going to visit them."

I stared at him. "You think she may have had a rendezvous with the person who killed her?"

"I don't necessarily think so, but it's possible. There's another angle: the killer might have known Janet was going to meet someone and struck before the rendezvous could be kept. The person Janet was going to meet could be holding his tongue to avoid suspicion."

He took his pipe out of his mouth and looked at it thoughtfully. "Naturally everyone has spent a good deal of time considering the possibilities. It *could* have happened in a dozen ways – if you're prepared to accept that any one of your friends and neighbours could be capable of murder. But I don't intend to start pointing fingers at people without the slightest shred of evidence."

"There's one thing standing in the way of assuming it was premeditated," I said slowly. "The fact that the car had a flat tyre."

He laughed shortly. "My dear girl, what could be easier than hammering a nail into a tyre to make it look as though the flat was the reason for pulling off the road?"

"Oh." I thought about it. "Yes, I see."

Tony got up and tapped the ashes out of his pipe into the grate.

"Well, there you have it. The killer could be a thug who saw a chance for a few quick dollars and grabbed it, and is now a thousand miles away. Or he – or she – could live here, on this orchard. Or he could live next door, or on one of the neighbouring orchards. Does it alter your decision to take this job?"

"Not in the least," I said firmly. "How could it possibly have anything to do with me?"

"I shouldn't think there could be the least possibility," Tony agreed. "But there is a chance there could be a murderer in the vicinity. I thought you should know that."

"Even if the murderer does live somewhere near," I said seriously, "He – or she – would hardly pose a threat to me unless he were a homicidal maniac. And somehow I don't think a homicidal maniac would bother to empty the poor girl's handbag to make a mad crime look like a brutally sane one. Do you?"

"No," Tony agreed quietly. "I don't think it was the work of a madman, either."

Tony went off about his work on the orchard and I changed

into slacks and a sweater and spent an hour familiarizing myself with the house, trying to concentrate on the work I must do and shut my mind to the queer situation I had stumbled into.

The Gootches had a comfortable small house a hundred and fifty metres or so from the main house and Mrs Gootch, plump and fiftyish, was obviously pleased and relieved that the Maynards had secured a new housekeeper. She and her husband had lived on the orchard for fifteen years, she told me, and her husband was the orchard foreman, in charge of any labour employed for orchard work. Mrs Maynard had engaged him when her husband died and she needed a man of experience to do the practical running of the orchard.

"Mrs Maynard was quite able to handle the business side of it," Mrs Gootch explained, "but even then she was none too strong in her body."

"It's a wonder," I commented, "she didn't sell the orchard when Mr Maynard died."

Mrs Gootch seemed amused. "I don't think the idea every entered her head. She lived all her married life here. I don't think she *could* live anywhere else."

"I should think your husband might have felt a bit resentful when young Mr Maynard came and took over the running of the orchard," I suggested.

"Oh, no." She shook her head emphatically. "My Harry's still the foreman, and that's plenty of work and responsibility for him. Tony took over the business side of it, relieving his grandmother of the worry. It's a good arrangement."

"Mrs Maynard looks very frail," I commented.

Mrs Gootch nodded. "She's had several bad heart attacks, real bad ones. She's a wonderful old lady, but she could go off at any minute and that's a fact."

"Do you think Mr Maynard – Tony – came with the intention of staying?" I asked casually. "I mean, was it arranged before he came out from England?"

"Oh, no, it wasn't planned or anything. Mrs Maynard

didn't even know he was coming. He planned it as a surprise for her." Mrs Gootch shook her head. "It didn't quite turn out the way he intended, of course, but she's been so much happier since he came she's like a different person. Harry never thought Tony would take to orchard life – lived in towns all his life and didn't know the first thing about any kind of farming, though he was a motor mechanic by trade, and that's real handy with so much machinery around. But he knuckled down and learned the orchard business from the ground up. Nothing could have pleased the old lady more. She's that fond of him – though she's not overmuch one to to show her feelings. It would break her heart if he left now – not that he's likely to, not if he knows which side his bread's buttered. This is a valuable property."

I said, "You think Tony's likely to inherit the orchard?"

"What else?" Mrs Gootch answered cheerfully. "Mrs Maynard doesn't have any other family."

"I see," I said after a moment. "Then Tony would have inherited even if he'd still been in England?"

"Well –" She hesitated. "As to that, I couldn't say, I'm sure. But we always *felt*, Harry and I, that she might have left it to someone outside the family. Mind you, that's only guesswork. But family don't seem so important when they're on the other side of the world and you don't even know them."

"No," I agreed slowly, "I can believe that."

I walked thoughtfully back to the house. Certainly the obvious reason for the masquerade this man – whoever he was – was engaged in seemed to be a hope that he might inherit the orchard. And yet surely it was too risky.

It would be easy enough to turn up and announce to Margaret Maynard that he was the grandson she hadn't seen since he was two years old. But to convince the relevant authorities he was that man would be a very different matter. To inherit, he would have to produce proof of identity. And suppose the real Tony Maynard were to show up? That might not be probable but it was a possibility which had to be considered. This man was no fool. He must have taken all these things into consideration, and inheritance must be his objective.

It was the next afternoon when Mrs Maynard asked me if I would drive into the village to post letters. "Take my car, Anne – the little Honda. I don't expect you to use your own car to run errands for me."

I drove about three hundred metres between rows of apple trees on the Maynard orchard and then turned on to a sealed road. Orchards lay all around me, and the fences often were hedges of hawthorn or briar and were clearly efforts on the part of early settlers to bring a bit of the English countryside to this foreign land. And they had largely succeeded.

Suddenly I slammed on the brakes as a black bundle I had thought was an old coat on the roadside moved. I pulled off on to the verge and ran back.

A black and white Border collie lay scuffling feebly at the bitumen, blood oozing from a gash on his shoulder, his eyes glazed with shock and pain. I knelt beside him and spoke to him and he whimpered faintly, but as I reached out a hand to his head he bared white fangs in a snarl of savagery which I was sure was caused entirely by his agony, but which was no less dangerous for that.

"Poor fellow," I said crooningly. "Poor old fellow. Come on, now, let me help."

I went on with a string of endearments and good advice in the hope that a gentle monotone might reassure him enough to let me pick him up and get him into the car. I didn't even stop to wonder whether Mrs Maynard would approve blood and mud and dog hair in her car.

But every time I reached out to him the teeth bared and a deep growl rumbled in his throat.

I sat back on my heels and looked at him. As far as I could assess with totally inexpert eyes he had a broken hind leg, a bad gash on his ribs and another on his shoulder, and he could have only Heaven and a vet would know what other injuries, because there was blood in his mouth.

"Well, old chap," I said slowly, thinking aloud now as much as soothing him, "I'm afraid you're probably beyond any help and I guess if I had a grain of sense I'd go back and get Mr Gootch to bring a gun and end it all for you. But maybe you've got a fighting chance. So you'll just have to let me get some sort of hold on you so I can put you in the car and get you to a vet."

I went to the car and opened a door to the back seat. I would have to grab the dog by the skin on the back of his neck to keep him from sinking his teeth into me. Then somehow I'd have to scoop him up with the other arm and hope my grip on his neck held, because any movement would hurt him dreadfully and he would naturally try to bite in what he saw as self-defence.

As I got back to him I heard a car approaching and looked up eagerly.

Then my heart sank as I realized the car was coming out of a side road which joined this road a hundred metres ahead. The chances were that whoever was driving it would simply turn toward Hobart and be gone before I could intercept to ask for help – if he or she could be persuaded to help.

A white station-wagon came out from between trees and paused while the driver checked for traffic. I waved and pointed at the dog and the station-wagon shot towards me, braked hard to a halt and the driver leapt out and ran across the road.

He stopped short when he saw the collie. For a moment he just stood staring like a man who has seen a ghost, and then he rubbed one hand over his face as it to wipe the apparition away.

"A dog!" he said. "My God, for a minute I thought –"

He stopped and looked at me. "I – I'm sorry," he said hastily.

And suddenly I knew why he had looked the way he had. For a moment he thought history had repeated itself, and another body lay by the roadside. It must, after all, have been somewhere near here that Janet Chisholm's body had been found.

"Is it your dog?" he asked. "He looks in bad shape."

I shook my head. "I just came along and found him. He needs help and he's vicious with pain and won't let me touch him. I wonder if you could help me get him into the car so I can take him to a vet?"

The man went down on one knee beside the crippled collie, talking to it much as I had, ignoring moist earth on neatly-pressed slacks. He was tall, about the same height as Tony Maynard, and his hair, like Tony's, was fair and wavy. But there the resemblance ended. This man was probably five years older and much more slender in build, though his sun-browned skin suggested the leanness was probably toughly wiry. His voice was quiet and steady as he talked to the dog, and to my surprise the tormented animal allowed him to lay a hand on its head and gently fondle its ears.

The man turned his head to look at me. "Isn't that Mrs Maynard's car?"

I nodded. "I'm her new housekeeper. She asked me to take her car and post some letters for her in the village."

"I'm going into Hobart and I know where there's a good vet, so I'll take the dog if you like. If you take him, Mrs Maynard will wonder where you are."

"I hadn't thought of that," I admitted. "I just saw the dog and – well, I couldn't just go and leave him, could I?"

He smiled, a slow smile that flicked light in dreamy grey-blue eyes. "I see. Well, I'll see if I have some twine or something in the car."

He came back with a slightly greasy rag which he tore into a couple of strips and knotted together. "I'll have to gag him so he can't bite," he explained, slipping a loop of rag around the collie's muzzle and tying it. "It will hurt him to be moved and it's only natural he'll try to bite." He looked at me. "Do we know whose dog it is?"

"I certainly dont, but then I'm new here. It's not Buzz, the Maynards' dog."

The necessary question of the dog's ownership hadn't occurred to me.

"Well, I know most dogs around the district," the man said, "but I don't recognize this one. Don't worry, I'll pay the bill and give him a home if we can't find the owners. If he lives. Unless you'd like him?"

"But I don't see any reason why you should pay the vet's bill! It was my idea to stop and try to help."

"Well, let's sort it out later, Mrs –?"

"Baker," I said, relieved that I hadn't had to hesitate over the name. "Anne Baker. Miss."

He gave a strangely courteous little nod which I felt in another era would have become a bow. "I'm a neighbour – Ashley Maclean." He lifted the dog, which gave a half-stifled yelp of pain, and laid it carefully in the back of the station-wagon. "I'll let you know how he gets on."

He turned the station-sedan around deftly and was gone.

As I drove on to the post office I remembered the stunned look of horror on Ashley Maclean's face as he had leapt from his car. Had Janet Chisholm been a friend of his and his wife's?

I asked as much that evening of Tony and Mrs Maynard. The old lady liked to have dinner with Tony and me, I had learned, unless she was feeling particularly exhausted, and I had been telling them both the story of the injured collie.

"Janet was a friend of Ashley's," Tony said.

"There is no Mrs Maclean," Margaret Maynard put in. "Ashley is a widower."

"Grandma would have been tickled pink if Ashley and Janet had made a match of it," Tony declared, smiling at her.

"Ashley's parents were our neighbours and friends for years," Mrs Maynard explained. "They bought that orchard when they were first married, and Ashley grew up there. His wife died of leukaemia when they'd been married only four years. Ashley never really looked at another women until Janet came along – and I don't think they were any more than good friends who had a lot in common, a lot of shared interests, though I readily admit I'd have been delighted for Ashley's sake if something more had come of it. I was fond of Janet."

There was a little silence, and I turned to Tony. "Ashley Maclean offered to give the dog a home, if it lives and we can't find its owner. Do you have any idea whose dog it might be?"

Tony shook his head. "Most people have dogs. I can't think of anyone with a Border collie, off-hand." He looked at me with an amused twinkle in his blue eyes. "If Ashley hadn't been willing to give the dog a home, I'll bet you'd want to take it in."

"Probably," I agreed, and got up to begin clearing the table.

I was still washing up when I saw car-lights come along the drive through the orchard, but I took no notice of the voices in the loungeroom until Ashley Maclean spoke beside me as he picked up a tea-towel and began wiping dishes as if he were thoroughly accustomed to it.

"I thought you'd like to know about the dog," he said. "Well, the vet thinks he'll be all right. He's set the broken leg and stitched a couple of the worst cuts, but he doesn't think there are any serious internal injuries. The blood in his mouth was from a cut tongue – probably put a tooth through it."

He smiled at my pleasure and said, "Perhaps the nicest thing is that the dog's owner came looking for him this evening. He was stopping at every house near the road, asking if anyone had seen it. Apparently the dog was riding in the back of this fellow's pick-up and must have somehow overbalanced and fallen out, and the owner didn't realize the dog was missing till he got home. He remembered having had to swerve to miss a big lorry somewhere in this area, so he guessed that was where he'd lost his passenger. He asked me to thank you for what you did."

"I didn't do anything except wave for help," I pointed out. "But I'm very glad it had a happy ending."

He nodded. "Would you celebrate by letting me take you to a small party next Saturday evening? It's near here and at least you'd meet some of the neighbours."

I told him I'd be delighted, and meant it, especially since as well as giving me an opportunity to meet some more neighbouring people, it might also give me a chance to learn more from them about Tony Maynard.

The party was at the home of a middle-aged couple named Mason, who lived several orchards away.

"Oh, the Masons," Tony had said disinterestedly when I told him where I was going. "Shouldn't think the party would be much of a riot. Bit Churchy, the Masons."

"Tony!" Mrs Maynard objected sharply. "The Masons are very nice people. Being interested in Church affairs is not exactly detrimental to anyone's character and it would do you no harm to discover that."

"Sorry, Gran." He smiled at her with a charming touch of deference.

On the evening of the party, when I came out to the living-room in a long dress of dark blue wool which I knew was flattering to my colouring and figure, Tony came instinctively to his feet, eyeing me appreciatively.

"You look absolutely stunning," he said. "Pity to waste it on Ashley and the Masons."

"Meaning?" I asked.

He laughed. "With the possible exception of Janet Chisholm, Ashley's never noticed a woman since his wife died, apparently. And the Masons' idea of a lively evening will probably be dry sherry and Beethoven records. If I were taking out a girl who looks the way you look tonight, I'd be showing her off to half the city."

"Thank you," I said drily.

Mrs Maynard said a trifle tartly, "Then you should take Anne out yourself some evening."

Tony hadn't taken his eyes off me. "I might, at that," he said softly. "I just might."

Our eyes held for a long moment, and I was intensely aware of his good looks, his sheer masculine vitality, and that indefinable sense that this was an exciting man. Dangerous, perhaps, my brain warned me, and certainly devious. But unquestionably exciting.

The sound of Ashley's car in the driveway broke the moment and I said lightly as I went towards the door, "Never mind. I like Beethoven."

I wondered as I slipped into my coat whether Tony hadn't been as readily accepted by the neighbours as he would have liked, and he resented it and aired his grievance by sneering at the Masons and Ashley Maclean. Or perhaps he was just an inverted snob who scoffed at a love of classical music and good books and other things of culture, without in the least realizing that he was being exactly the kind of snob he was ready to accuse others of being.

Whatever lay under the surface of the man who called himself Tony Maynard, it was disturbing. By no means the least disturbing thing about him was the disarming quality of his charm when he chose to use it. And it might well be unwise to be disarmed, I reminded myself, when dealing with Tony Maynard.

Ashley's slow smile and quiet courtesy by contrast were as comfortable as slipping on an old pair of favourite shoes, and even as the thought occurred to me, I was aware of how contemptuously Tony would have been amused by it. Annoyed with myself, I told myself firmly I wouldn't think about him any more that evening.

The party was by no means as uninteresting as Tony had predicted, though he may have found it dull for his tastes, for all I knew of him. The first thing I discovered was that

Ashley Maclean, for all his quiet reserve, could be very good company. Or perhaps that was just because I was interested in what he had to say.

On the way to the Masons' house we drove over a small stone bridge and Ashley said, "This little bridge is one of the things we always tell visitors about. It's quite old." He smiled and raised one hand from the wheel in a little gesture of apology. "Not old in the sense you're used to in Britain with buildings galore that have stood for a whole string of centuries. But you have to remember in Australia that the European race have only been here for less than two hundred years, so things which seem relatively modern to you are old to us."

He shook his head and said quietly, "The things that were really old, we couldn't wait to destroy."

I said nothing, and he must have realized I didn't know what he meant.

"The aborigines had been here for thousands of years. So long that those here in Tasmania were in fact a slightly different race from those on the mainland. Probably they were people who belonged to the first race of aborigines to come into Australia by way of the so-called land-bridge from Asia, before that land sank and became a string of islands. The people we call the Australian aborigines came later – and they were technologically superior, if I might put it that way. They had better spears, they had the boomerang, and the woomera – a device for throwing spears farther and straighter. They had dogs – the dingo. And for the people without these things, retreat was inevitable. Tasmania became their last refuge. At least that's the theory many people hold, and I believe it's most probably correct. But the people here were a nuisance and they were usually wrongly regarded as sometimes a danger to the early white settlers, an impediment to the thing we call progress and civilization. So we wiped them out. Methodically, carefully, and very effectively."

"Surely not deliberately?" I objected.

He stopped the station-sedan outside a house ablaze with lights and with eight or ten cars parked beside it.

"Deliberately enough," he answered. "At least, by the time enough people had qualms about it, it was too late. They were gone. The last one to live in Tasmania was an old lady who died over a century ago."

His hands rested on the steering-wheel for a moment after he parked and switched off the engine.

"Awesome, isn't it?" he said, his profile grave as he looked at the brightly-lit house. In that moment I felt he saw, backwards in time, the island that was his home struggling through many torments, many blunders, as every nation struggles. "A whole race of people, unique on the earth, wiped out – the people, their beliefs, language, customs – all gone, as if they had never existed, and it only took us Europeans eighty-five years and a lot of excuses. Two thousand people whose only crime was that we didn't understand them, gone. Vanished, through greed and ignorance and intolerance. And fear. Fear is the greatest destroyer of all. We always want to destroy the things we're afraid of. That's why the history of our treatment of the convicts who settled this country is so grim, too. Their jailors were afraid of them"

"That bridge back there – the one you said was old. Was that built by convicts?" I asked.

He nodded. "There were skilled craftsmen among them, and they left us some wonderfully artistic buildings and bridges. Quite beautiful things, created by men in chains. Sometimes I wonder whether the lovely, simple lines of the things they built gave them any kind of a sense of achievement, of creativity; or whether all they built into those stones was hate."

He looked at me suddenly and smiled. "Anne, what a shocking bore I am! I'm supposed to be taking you to a party, not lamenting at length on all the sad things in our history. And it isn't all brutality and misery, not by any means. There are wonderful achievements, too. And I'm not going to say another serious word all evening. Come."

He leapt out of the car and came around to my door. "I wasn't bored. Quite the reverse," I told him. "I find the whole fact that Australia was founded as a prison colony quite fascinating. Grim and horrible in many respects – the history of every country is – and yet it's inspiring, too. I mean the basic fact that a whole new nation grew out of a prison camp. It's a monumental example of the resilience of the human spirit."

We were walking toward the house as we spoke, and in a minute Ashley was introducing me to the Masons, and the moment of seriousness was gone. But I found myself watching him as he talked to people with that quiet courtesy which was so natural to him and which obviously made him popular with these people, and I realized that behind the sensitive, almost dreamy face there was a man with deep and intense feelings. A strong man, I thought suddenly. I found myself thinking of Tony Maynard and unconsciously comparing the two, though they were so very different. Certainly Ashley lacked the kind of glittering excitement that lay just under the surface in Tony. But both, I thought, had depths about their characters it might be hard to plumb. Two strong men. Both might be capable of surprising things.

All the guests at the party were people who lived in the neighbourhood, though at least two couples, I discovered, were not orchardists, but worked in Hobart. "It's a very strong trend these days," our host explained as he introduced me, "for people to get out of town and buy a bit of land to give them a little breathing-space. Much of the land around here will ultimately become residential instead of orchard land."

Vera Mason was a plain woman with a happy effervescence which was even more appealing than the cool loveliness of the tall young woman she introduced to me as Lesleigh Martin.

Slender, with shoulder-length gleaming copper-red hair,

Lesleigh Martin had the kind of looks no man who still had breath in his body could fail to notice and admire, and no woman could fail to envy.

"Lesleigh and her two brothers have bought an orchard quite near Fairfield, the Maynard orchard," Vera Mason explained. "Lesleigh works on it, right along with the men. Gave up a first-class job as private secretary to a Parliamentarian a couple of years ago to come farming, and she does it most efficiently."

"That's very interesting," I said somewhat lamely, and must have looked as surprised as I felt. Lesleigh Martin the private secretary I could see. Lesleigh Martin driving a tractor or up a ladder with a canvas bag slung around her neck, picking apples, I could not see.

"Oh, it's perfectly true," Lesleigh said calmly, reading my face. "People always think women who work on farming jobs have to be horse-faced and weigh fourteen stone and be barely able to read and write. God knows why."

Her light brown eyes swept me appraisingly. Vera Mason had smilingly excused herself to see to other guests. "You're Janet Chisholm's successor, aren't you?" Lesleigh asked.

"And housekeepers are supposed to be plump and over forty and call everybody 'dearie'," I suggested.

She nodded. "Something like that. Why are you doing it?"

The bluntness of the question might have sounded rude from most people, but coming from Lesleigh Martin it somehow seemed perfectly natural.

"I've been a teacher for six years. I thought I'd like a change of occupation."

"And do you like it?"

"I've only been doing it for a fortnight. But yes, so far I do. What made you give up such an interesting job?" I asked brightly. "Secretary to a Member of Parliament must be quite fascinating – much more exciting than working on an orchard."

"All intrigue and State secrets? Sorry to disappoint you," Lesleigh said drily, "but my Member wasn't the type. Any more than you're the type to settle for a housekeeping job. But I suppose it's only temporary – a means of working your passage while you have a look at Australia?"

"I suppose so," I agreed noncommittally. It occurred to me that this might be an opportunity to learn something more from an outsider about the household I was involved in. "So it seems," I said carefully, "a number of people don't run true to type. What about Janet Chisholm? Was she more your type of person to be in a housekeeping job?"

Lesleigh's face went strangely hard. "This is a polite household we're in," she said, "or I'd tell you the kind of job Janet Chisholm was most suited for."

I blinked, completely taken back by the reply. "Mrs Maynard liked her very well," I said protestingly, "and I should think she'd be rather particular about her companions."

"Very likely. I imagine Janet showed only her best side to the Maynards, since they paid her wages. Just as she showed only her best side to Ashley Maclean."

There was a little pause, and I though uncomfortably that I knew now why Lesleigh Martin had been interested in me. Ashley had brought me to this party. Ashley had been friendly with Janet Chisholm. And Lesleigh was interested in Ashley.

Before I could think of anything to say, Lesleigh asked, "Who is staying with Mrs Maynard while you have a night out – Tony?"

I nodded, and remembered that I had thought this party might give me some idea of how the people in the district regarded Tony Maynard. Lesleigh Martin would be a keen observer of human inter-reactions; her opinion of him might be interesting.

"Mrs Maynard is certainly fond of Tony," I said. "It was very fortunate he came, and settled into orchard life as he has."

Lesleigh sipped her drink, looking at me over the glass. "It was fortunate for Tony."

"What do you mean?"

"My dear girl! The man turns up, a penniless motor-mechanic out of a job – at least, I assume the penniless part; his car was something of a rust-bucket, I gather. And he walks on to a valuable piece of property with every prospect of becoming heir to it. Of course he toes the line and is everything his grandmother could wish him to be. He'd be an idiot if he played it any other way."

"So you think he's playing a part – an acting role?"

She heard the real interest in my tone and looked at me a shade curiously. "Yes," she said after a moment's consideration. "I think he is."

"He works very hard," I said.

"Oh, he does," she agreed. "He's been almost as wonderful as his grandmother believes. Good luck to him. From the way he's worked, and been so nice to the old lady, he deserves to have the place."

And somewhere inside me, some entirely practical, reasoning part of me agreed. He deserved to have the place. And yet –

"Tony seems to me," I said, "a quite remarkable man."

She looked amused. "Quite. You're not falling for him, are you? It's very easy to fall for Tony Maynard. But my dear, you strike me as being too sweet and innocent to be involved with someone like him."

It was my turn to be amused at the thought of Lesleigh Martin endeavouring to protect me. But I was interested, too.

"Why?" I asked. "What is Tony Maynard like?"

She shrugged. "He just strikes me," she said indifferently, "as the kind of man who has something very hard inside him. And as for women, he'd be perfectly happy to swear undying love and devotion to anything female, just to get himself a pleasant weekend diversion."

I laughed. "That part I can well believe. I *have* met the type before, I assure you. But –"

"Anne, I'm a frightfully poor escort," Ashley's voice said beside me. "Mrs Bonnington buttonholed me to tell me in rather considerable detail about a concert she and her husband had flown to Sydney to attend. Hello, Lesleigh." He smiled at her. "You're looking very beautiful, as always."

It was said with simple admiration.

"Thank you," Lesleigh said easily, and looked at me. "You should see me in my working gear some time, and then you'd know he's a liar. Did the Bonningtons really fly to Sydney to a *concert*? Good Lord. Tell me, Anne, are *you* flipped on Bach Fugues and things? Mrs Maynard's very keen on classical music, I know – when she and Ashley get together it's like listening to people talking a foreign language. If it isn't music it's the garden. They go around introducing every leafy thing by its botanical name – at least that's what they say. I've wondered at times if they're not really saying something naughty in Latin. Janet Chisholm was quite adept at the same things. I wondered if it was a required skill for all Mrs Maynard's companions."

I felt uncomfortably that Lesleigh had tossed Janet's name into the conversation simply to watch Ashley's reaction. He showed none.

I said quickly, "I like classical music, though I certainly couldn't pretend to be as knowledgeable as Mrs Maynard. And I *can* chat about plants by their botanical names – solely because I once had an elderly landlord who would insist on dragging me around his garden by the hour, lecturing me on how he'd got his chaenomeles flowering so well this winter, or showing me where he'd planted colchiums under the syringa. Some of it rubbed off on me."

Ashley laughed and Lesleigh gave a melodramatic sigh. "I am routed. Utterly defeated. Ashley will never look at me while you're about. Do you do normal, human, unlearned things like riding horses or playing golf?"

"I play a bit of golf."

"Good. We must have a game one day soon. There's quite a good course not far from here."

She moved away to speak to someone else, and for a moment Ashley watched her, his face shuttered and expressionless, and I wondered if he was thinking of Lesleigh or of Janet. It was strange, I reflected: for all her casually outspoken manner, I would not have thought Lesleigh Martin an unkind person; yet she had spoken bitterly and without a trace of regret or sympathy for a woman who so recently had been brutally murdered.

Then Ashley turned to me and began to talk, and drew me into conversation with a group of people, and the ghost of Janet Chisholm seemed to recede.

It was only a good deal later in the evening that anyone spoke of her. Most of the people present seemed to know Margaret Maynard, and it was obvious she was liked and respected. Tony also seemed quite well-liked. Certainly those who were orchardists clearly admired the way he worked and the manner in which he'd tackled learning the business. But I gained the distinct impression that, for all that, no one really knew him.

It was the plump and jovial Mr Bonnington of the fly-to-Sydney-to-a-concert episode who talked to me about Janet Chisholm. A chatty little man made more so by a fair intake of whisky, he sought me out with a cheery, "Well, my dear, I've been wanting to speak to you all evening. Look, there are two vacant chairs, so do let's grab 'em."

He dropped into one with a sigh of relief. "That's the trouble with parties. Always three times as many people as there are chairs, and when you get to my age and weight the feet object very strongly. It's the *only* trouble with parties, though. I love 'em."

He beamed at me through rimless glasses and I smiled back, instinctively liking him.

"You work for Mrs Maynard, I believe – her new companion?"

"I'm more housekeeper than anything else."

"Uh-huh. Not your usual kind of job, though, is it?"

"I'm a teacher." I had grown used to the local curiosity about my background. "I was looking for a change of job for a while."

Mr Bonnington nodded. "Fine woman, Mrs Maynard. Not that my wife and I know her so very well – we've only lived here three years – retired, you know – and Mrs Maynard wasn't well even when we came, and never got about very much. But on those times when we have met, we liked her. A – a *lady*, if you know what I mean."

I did know, and I nodded. "Yes. She must have a fine spirit, to go on managing the orchard after she became ill, right up until her grandson came."

I threw out the bait but found I was not going to learn anything about Tony from Mr Bonnington. But of course, never having been an orchardist he wouldn't be likely to know Tony. He dismissed him with, "Yes, I guess she was pleased when he turned up." He sipped his whisky. "I think it would be harder for her to hand over the running of her house than to hand over the running of her orchard. A house becomes a very personal thing to a woman. Very personal. To have to give up running it –" He shrugged. "It'd be a kind of admission of defeat, I guess. I shouldn't think Mrs Maynard would like that."

I hadn't thought of it like that, and I looked at Mr Bonnington with respect. I didn't think Margaret Maynard would like admitting defeat, either.

"Of course, she was lucky with Janet Chisholm, too," he said.

I reflected that I'd heard a lot of people talk about Janet, and yet I knew very little about her. "What was she like?" I asked.

"Janet?" He looked thoughtful. "Quiet. Unobtrusive kind of person. Always gave me the impression there was something under the surface – as though there was a good deal more to Janet Chisholm than met the eye. Seemed a nice person, though she double-dealt Ashley Maclean fast enough when it suited her. Maybe it didn't matter to him – Ashley's not the kind to let anyone know what he feels."

I said nothing, doing some rapid thinking. Apparently people took it for granted that Ashley's friendship with Janet had been serious. And apparently she had been hitting it off with someone else at the same time.

"Must have made Ashley something of a prime suspect with the police, I suppose, though really there was nothing to say he and Janet were anything but good friends. He took her out a bit, that's all." He chuckled. "I'd have thought he might have preferred Lesleigh Martin. Certainly would have if looks had anything to do with it. Spirit, too, I'd think – Lesleigh has plenty of that. Yet, like I said, there was always the feeling there was more to Janet than you'd think on first acquaintance. Still water running deep, and all that. Certainly no secret to anyone with eyes in their head that Lesleigh went off the deep end over Ashley for a while."

"For a while," I echoed. "Not any more, then?"

"Eh? Oh, Lesleigh. No, shouldn't think so. Certainly doesn't appear to be interested in him, or not seriously, now. I'd say she probably decided she and Ashley weren't really compatible. Lesleigh likes horses and fast cars and all that sort of thing. Ashley'd rather music and books and stuff like that. Though mark you, I believe he was a top-notch cricketer, once – would have got to play for Australia, they say, if he hadn't given it up because he had too much to do on the orchard. Even now, I've seen him bowl a real mean ball on a rare occasion when they've persuaded him to play club cricket. What I meant is, he's more the intellectual type than Lesleigh."

"Lesleigh," I commented, "strikes me as being anything but dull, intellectually."

Mr Bonnington grinned. "Oh, I grant you Lesleigh is a very smart girl. But she's packed with a kind of nervous energy that drives her to charge off at all sorts of physical pursuits. Ashley's a much quieter type. That's all I meant."

There was still a light in Fairfield when Ashley drove me home, and as I went into the livingroom Tony came out of the office and I got the impression he had deliberately waited up for me. I wondered whether he was curious to know if anyone had talked about him, and what they might have said.

"Well," he said with a smile, "how was the party?"

"Very pleasant," I told him. "And Beethoven didn't even raise his tousled head. You're working late."

He yawned. "Got engrossed in the books. Would you like some coffee?"

"No, thank you," I said. "I'm a bit tired." I had some thinking to do, and I had no wish to become involved in a post-mortem of someone else's party with Tony Maynard.

Four

Drew Thomas came to stay for the weekend.

He was seventeen, black-haired and brown-eyed, of a slender but athletic build that promised to develop. A lively final-year high-school student, he was as delightful as a breath of cool breeze on a stifling summer day, and I fell for him as if he had been the young brother I'd never had.

Mrs Maynard had been obviously delighted when Drew had telephoned to ask if he could come for the weekend. He parked his dilapidated Volkswagen and greeted her with genuine warmth and me with cheerfully frank curiosity, and then set to work on the orchard promptly and with enthusiasm, and it was clear that he had often worked there before.

Tony had been in the house having a quick cup of coffee on the Friday afternoon when Drew arrived, and he greeted him in a perfectly polite and friendly manner and, as soon as Drew changed his high-school uniform for jeans and boots and a heavy sweater against a grey and overcast afternoon, the two strode off companioningly together to work – Drew full of questions about exactly what was being done on the orchard at the moment, and Tony answering readily.

Yet I felt that somehow there was an underlying hostility in Tony toward the boy, though it wasn't something I could pinpoint.

It was patently obvious that Drew loved being at Fairfield and he was horrified when I admitted I hadn't yet been all over the property.

Although I certainly didn't say so, in the short time I'd been there I had been too determined to consolidate my position, by being as much the perfect houskeeper-companion as possible, to take any time out for exploring, except for the immediate surroundings such as the machinery and packing sheds.

Drew regarded this as a woeful lack of natural curiosity which almost amounted to an insult to Fairfield and, as such, intolerable. "Haven't you even walked down to the Channel?" he demanded.

I shook my head and smiled. "Young man, some of us have to *work* for a living."

He pulled a face. "But not all the time! Mrs Maynard won't mind if you go out for an hour or so, will you, Mrs M.?"

She smiled. "Of course not. Anne, you mustn't feel bound to stay in the house all the time. I'm perfectly all right left alone occasionally, I assure you. Go along with Drew and let him show you the place properly."

We walked down through the blossoming trees to where the orchard met the water of the D'Entrecasteaux Channel, and he showed me that the orchard was not the whole of Fairfield. It also encompassed a smallish timbered area and some pastures where white dots of woolly sheep grazed, like tiny puffs of cloud in an emerald sky.

We came back past the farm sheds, and a little beyond them, three tiny wooden cottages, closed and empty.

"Accommodation for the seasonal workers," Drew told me. "The place really comes to life in the fruit-picking season, and extra hands have to be put on, beginning about the middle of January. They live in these huts and cook their own meals and everything."

I looked around at the cottages and the sheds, almost completely hidden from the house by the stand of trees which formed a back-drop for the house as one came up to it from the road.

"Whoever planned the layout of trees and buildings and gardens here was quite an artist at landscape design," I said.

Drew nodded. "Wasn't he? Nothing so mundane as a packing shed would be tolerated unless it took its proper place. Out of sight. He left the best of the native bush and added his English imports. You'll see the same idea carried out again at Oakhill."

"Oakhill?"

"Ashley Maclean's place. According to the old records – the deeds and things – the two places were taken up originally by the same settler, and Ashley's place was given to the original owner's son."

"Are the Maynards or the Macleans descended from the original owners?"

"Oh, no. Mrs Maynard's husband was only the second generation of his family to own Fairfield, and Ashley is only the second generation of *his* family on Oakhill."

He stopped as we came in sight of the house and stood for a moment, his young face intent as he looked at the house, and beyond it to where the water lapped the shore as it curved northward toward Hobart.

"Fancy anyone who owned a place like this selling it," he said softly. Then he grinned and looked faintly embarrassed. "I promised Tony I'd mend a fence, so I'd better go and do it if I don't want to wear out my welcome on the place."

"Is Tony the boss?" I asked casually.

Drew shot me a look. "No way. *And* he knows it. I think it rather riles him sometimes that a frail old lady keeps tabs on him so closely. There's very little goes on at Fairfield Mrs Maynard doesn't know about, and she still makes the final decisions on all the major things. But you can hardly blame her for keeping hold of the reins, can you?"

I remarked to Mrs Maynard next morning that I had rather fallen for Drew.

She smiled. "I'm glad of that. I fell for him a long time ago. There's something fresh and unspoiled about him and always has been. One keeps hoping it won't change with age. His grandparents were friends of ours for many years – his grandfather was my husband's solicitor – and Drew regards coming out here for a weekend or for school holidays in much the same way as most boys would regard sport – a complete change from study, and therefore relaxation."

She looked thoughtful. "Before Tony came, Drew's visits were one of the few bright spots in my life, after I became restricted by this silly thing." She tapped her chest.

She was sitting in the easy chair in her room, where she had had her breakfast, with Percy the black cat curled on her lap, and Butch, the black-and-white cat washing herself on the rug in front of the fireplace. Butch, I had been told, was named in infancy in the mistaken belief it was male. I drew the curtains fully open. The grey overcast of the previous day had been swept away by a steady west wind and the sun poured brightly over a world fully awakened into spring. The azaleas in the garden were splashes of colour along the drive and the ornamental cherries were a mass of bloom, while the sweep of orchard we could see from the window frothed with blossom.

Behind me, Mrs Maynard said softly, "I would have

been forced to give it all up, if Tony hadn't come."

I turned and saw she was gazing out of the window, her eyes alight with joy at the beauty of the scene.

"I kept pretending to myself that I could cope, with Harry Gootch's help," she went on, "but I was only trying to turn a blind eye to the truth. The management, the business side of it, was getting beyond my strength."

"Tony's coming was most fortunate," I said carefully.

She nodded. "Even though it was in such sad circumstances, it was a great joy to me – and continued to be. You see, Anne, Tony is virtually all the family I have left now. I was an only child, and so was my husband, and our two children died very much too young, each having had only one child. My son – Tony's father – and his wife were killed in an accident, and my daughter died of a sudden illness."

She looked down at the cat on her lap. "I do have a granddaughter somewhere in England – my daugher's child – but evidently she cares little for family ties. Few young people do these days. I used to write to her, after her father died, but she had moved away and my letters were returned. I haven't heard of her now for years. In all fairness she probably doesn't know where I live, or even whether I'm still alive, for that matter."

I turned quickly to look out of the window, my hands tight on the sill. I had no wish to have Margaret Maynard see my face at that moment.

"That's how families simply come to an end sometimes," she was saying. "Now, with a grandchild on Fairfield and taking such a lively interest in the place, it's like seeing our family line regenerated, given another chance. Do you know what I mean?"

I stood looking down at the beauty of Fairfield, feeling the intensity of pride in it that filled the frail old lady behind me.

"Yes," I said when I could trust my voice, "I know what you mean." I hesitated. "Had you kept in touch with Tony regularly before he came out here?"

"Oh, no. That is, I wrote occasionally to what was to me his last known address, but I'm afraid he didn't reply – a card once or twice at Christmas, that was all. But my letters weren't returned, so I assumed he got them. Indeed, he tells me he did."

I wasn't able to resist saying, "So he wasn't really much more thoughtful than your granddaughter."

"He didn't seem to be. That's why his arrival here was such a surprise. Of course, for some reason one doesn't expect a boy to take as much interest in his family as a girl might."

I risked asking, "Do you think he came here with the intention of staying?"

Do you think he came with the intention of worming his way into Fairfield, would have been a more accurate way of phrasing my question. Perhaps she guessed it.

"I think there was much more feeling for his family ties in Tony than I had previously credited him with. The azaleas are coming out quite beautifully, aren't they? The rhododendrons should be lovely in a little while, but they are later in flowering."

And so any discussion of Tony's motives was closed. I went out feeling bitterly angry. Tony the cherished and thoughtful grandson. Anne Beaconsfield the uncaring granddaughter. It didn't help to remind myself that I *hadn't* cared. The fact remained that since I had met Margaret Maynard, I *did* care. I cared rather a lot.

Neither did it help to remind myself that, whoever the man who called himself Tony Maynard really was, he had given the old lady joy and companionship, and had relieved her of most of her business worries. And I must hold my tongue.

As I strode out into the garden, prepared to vent my feelings on any weed that came to hand, I almost collided with Drew Thomas coming in.

"Hello," he said, looking startled. "Something wrong?"

"No," I said shortly. Then I pulled myself up and looked at his face blank with astonishment at the rudeness of my tone. "Sorry, Drew. I was just being bad-tempered over something."

I saw he was holding one hand as if it hurt him. "What have you done to your hand?"

"Oh, nothing really. Just clumsy enough to run a splinter into it off an old fence-post. I was coming in to look for something to get it out. It's not all that sore – just a nuisance."

"Do you want me to try my hand at getting it out for you?"

"Would you mind? It's in my right hand, and my mother always tells me I'm as handy as a pig with a pitchfork when I'm using a needle."

I laughed. "All right. Sit there on the garden seat in the sun while I gather up the necessary tools."

He said as I carefully removed a fairly nasty splinter, swabbed the area and applied adhesive tape, "You're a teacher by profession, aren't you? I guess you're used to patching up kids' minor injuries. You do it with a practised hand."

"Thanks. I did a basic first-aid course, but I've never been called on to deal with anything much more major than splinters or gravel-rash or the odd black eye. Oh, yes, two broken arms and an epileptic fit."

He pulled a face. "I've always planned on being a teacher myself, but you're putting me off. How in the dickens do you deal with an epileptic fit? Hell!" he added with quiet violence.

I looked up quickly, thinking he must have hurt his hand. But he was staring down the drive at an approaching police car.

And at once I felt the chill of remembering the thing that

was relatively easy for me to forget, but must be very much in the minds of the people closer to it: violent murder had been done here, and the murderer was not caught.

Two men in lounge suits got out of the car and came toward us, and I went forward to meet them. "Good morning. I'm Anne Baker, the housekeeper. I'm afraid Mr Maynard's out in the orchard, but I think –"

"Thank you, but it's young Mr Thomas we were wanting to see," the older man answered.

I glanced at Drew, who sat unmoving on the garden-seat, his young face serious and troubled. "Do sit down, Inspector," he said with easy flippancy which was clearly an act. "I've been expecting you."

And something in his manner told me he had.

I busied myself with indoor chores instead of going back into the garden. I felt as unhappy as Drew had looked. Why did the police want to see him? He had, I knew, been here when Janet Chisholm was killed, but the police must have asked all their routine questions then. Why had they come back?

Then I remembered what Tony had said when he had told me about the murder: 'They still come around occasionally, asking more questions – or the same questions over again to see if they get the same answers.'

This, I told myself, was police routine. But for some reason, Drew was unhappy about it. Well, wasn't that normal? No, I decided; the average seventeen-year-old, no more involved in this case than Drew should have been as a casual visitor, would have found the prospect of police questioning positively exciting.

Presently I heard the car drive away, and I went out into garden to begin my delayed attack on the weeds, even though my frame of mind had changed.

Drew was still sitting on the seat, exactly as he had been.

"It's all right," he said, seeing the surprise on my face. "They resisted the temptation to arrest me."

"Oh," I said cheerfully. "I notice they sent an inspector,

no less. Do you rob a bank after school *every* Friday?"

He shook his head. "Only during months ending in 'R'." He made a restless movement, immediately serious. "I was here when Janet was killed."

I nodded. "I'm sorry. It must have been grim. The police have to keep asking questions. Of everyone."

He hesitated, then shrugged. "I guess so. But I think something must have made them think I knew more than I was telling them. Otherwise why come back and start asking the same questions all over again? Although," he added moodily, "I knew they would."

I waited a moment. "*Do* you know something you haven't told them?" I asked quietly. "Because I hate to tell you this, old chap, but you're a rotten actor. When that police car showed, you looked as guilty as if you'd been caught leaving the Tower of London with half the Crown Jewels stuffed down your shirt-front. I imagine the look wasn't lost on them. I think whatever it is you know, you should tell them."

"No!" he said sharply.

"Why not?" I asked gently.

"Because it would look so bad, and it can't mean anything – not anything significant. It *can*'t. He's much too nice a fellow – he just wouldn't kill somebody. I mean – not *kill* somebody. Anyway, at one time he was keen on her, or so everyone thought; though I suppose the police might only think that was the very thing that could give him a motive. They *do* think that already, because they sure put him through hoops at the time. And he hasn't the ghost of an alibi."

I stared at Drew. "Who? Who are you talking about? Is it Tony?"

"Tony? Oh, Lord, no." He shook his head. "Tony'd no reason to kill her. No, not Tony. Ashley Maclean."

I sat down rather abruptly on the garden seat beside him, feeling my knees suddenly wouldn't support me. "Ashley Maclean," I echoed stupidly.

"He owns the orchard next door," Drew explained. "His wife died years ago and he lives alone, with a woman coming in daily to houseclean and everything. He and Janet were friends – he used to take her out and she'd go over to his place and they'd play records – things like that."

"Yes," I said. "I know." There was a little silence. "I thought," I said slowly, "any suggestion of a romance had been ended."

"Oh, it was." Drew frowned. "Janet switched her attention to somebody else. They went to this party, she and Ashley, and this guy was there and she just dropped Ashley like a hot stone and went for the other bloke and never looked at Ashley again. Must have been upsetting for him. Janet was like that."

Janet was like that.

Drew Thomas was the third person to indicate a none-too-warm opinion of Janet Chisholm. From Mrs Maynard – and, to a lesser degree, from Tony – I had heard nothing but praise of Janet. Obviously not everyone shared that high opinion. Outsiders saw Janet Chisholm the woman, not Janet Chisholm the devoted employee; and the two were different, as so often happens.

"Who was this other man?"

"Oh, some businessman. In food-processing or something. Good-looking enough bloke, and had money, of course." Drew looked at me. "Oh, I see: you're wondering about him as a suspect. No way, I'm afraid. He had a cast-iron alibi – he was in America."

We sat for a while without speaking. Then I said, "Drew, will you tell me why you think Ashley Maclean may have killed Janet?"

"I didn't say that! I *don't* think he killed her."

"You don't *want* to think he killed her," I said gently. "But you think he might have. Because she'd dropped him for this other man?"

"No," he said, and then added quickly, "I mean, that was months before."

"Was there another reason?"

"No, of course not." He shot me a troubled look.

"But you know something, don't you?" I persisted quietly. "Everyone knew about the other man. But you know something else."

"I don't *know* anything!" he said hotly. "It's just – well, just that it would *look* bad for him, that's all."

"Drew," I told him, "I like Ashley, too."

He looked hard at me, and then nodded. "I see. I've never told anybody, not even Mrs Maynard or my family. But I think you'd be the sort who knows how to keep quiet, and not go hounding a man about being a good citizen and doing the right thing. How do I know what the right thing is, anyway?"

I was oddly touched.

"I went for a walk," Drew explained, "the morning after Janet was killed, only of course none of us knew anything about it then – didn't even know she was missing. She'd gone out in her car the night before, but the way I sleep she could have come in and out a dozen times in a Centurion tank and I wouldn't have heard her. I woke up early when Tony got up, and decided I'd like to go for a walk, so I did. I let Buzz the dog off the chain and we went off together. I went across our – I mean, across this orchard, and through Ashley's."

I gave no sign I'd noticed that he'd spoken of Fairfield as if he were one of the family.

"So," he went on, "because I didn't go around by the road, I didn't see anything of Janet or her car. Her body couldn't be seen from the road, actually, because it was on the far side of the car. The truck-driver who found it was moved to investigate because he'd passed that way during the night and noticed the car, and when he came by again about day-break he saw the car was still there, and the driver's window was open, and he reckoned anyone leaving a broken-down car would have wound up all the windows and locked the car."

He stooped down to pick up a pebble and sat tossing it from one hand to the other. "I walked a mile or so, cutting across orchards and open land. On the way back I passed close by Ashley's house and the various orchard buildings clustered behind it. As I came towards the house I saw Ashley come out with a bundle of cloth in his hands and put it down beside the incinerator. Then he went back and brought out a bottle of what I'd say by the look of the bottle was kerosene, and a bundle of crumpled-up newspaper."

Drew stopped flicking the pebbled back and forth and just sat staring at it in the palm of his hand.

"I was still among the trees, and Ashley hadn't seen me, and I didn't even think there might be anything odd about a fellow burning a bundle of rags. I was just about to call a hello, but something in the way he handled those rags stopped me, and I just stood still and watched. He unfolded them carefully, and I could see they weren't rags at all. There was a perfectly good wool jacket and a scarf. Ashley stood for what seemed a long time, examing the clothes And I stared too, feeling a bit thunderstruck. Because I was close enough to see that both the coat and the scarf were heavily stained with blood!"

"Blood!" I exclaimed. "But – are you sure?"

"I've asked myself that," he said disconsolately, "a hundred times, and the answer, of course, is that I can't absolutely *know* that it was blood. No one could know it unless they had it analysed. All I know is that I felt very queer indeed when I saw it, and I didn't know then that there'd been a murder, so the old imagination wasn't so likely to go running riot as if I had known. I told myself it was animal blood – that he'd been handling an injured animal, or had had to kill one."

"Well, surely that's the most likely explanation?"

He shook his head. "That wouldn't explain why he'd want to burn the clothes. Why not put them in the garbage if they were beyond cleaning? Clothes are pretty hard things to burn. There was something about the whole situation that made me awfully glad Buzz had gone on ahead and wasn't on hand to go bounding up to Ashley Maclean and give away the fact that I was there. I remembered that some time in the course of my walk I'd heard a siren, like a police or ambulance siren. It had hardly even registered at the time, but when I saw the clothes I remembered, though I tried to tell myself it was crazy to think there was any connection. But I was suddenly awfully anxious Ashley should never know I'd seen those clothes."

I looked at Drew's face, and presently I asked, "Did you see what he did? I mean, did he really burn them?"

"He cut the buttons off the coat and put it and the scarf and the papers in the incinerator and poured kerosene over them."

He paused. "I cleared off home at that point, and found Grandma making herself a cup of tea because Janet wasn't up. That was unusual, so I went and knocked on her door. She didn't answer, so I went in – the door wasn't locked – and her bed was made and there was no sign of her. I remembered the siren and the clothes Ashley had, and I began to feel funny. Tony said her car wasn't in the garage, and almost before we had time to begin wondering, the police came. They asked us all questions – questions on questions. Naturally they wanted to know why I'd gone for a walk just after daylight on a very cold morning, and why I hadn't gone around the road – *if* I hadn't gone around the road, because of course they had only my word for that. Oddly enough, I had the feeling even then that they didn't think I'd killed Janet, but they did think I was hiding something, though they never said as much. I held my tongue over what I'd seen because I can't quite believe Ashley is a murderer."

I sat silent. My instincts told me the same thing; but cold hard logic told me it was damning evidence indeed.

Drew raised his head and looked at me gravely, his eyes troubled.

"Look here, Anne, I'm darned if I know why I told you about this. I've never told a soul. Not a word. Please, leave it, huh? I still don't believe Ashley did it. But – well, I can't *know*, can I? If there's any risk he *did* do it, I should tell what I saw. Because I guess it's true what they say: a murderer who goes free can kill again, either to protect his secret or because he's come to the conclusion he has some kind of special right to decide who should live and who should die – that sort of stuff."

"Did the police say that to you?"

"More or less." He ran a hand through his hair. "But it's my decision whether or not to tell about what I saw. And right or wrong, I have to make it myself. Okay?"

I took a very long breath. "All right, Drew. I don't really know, any more than you do, whether what you're doing is right or wrong. I'll hold my tongue."

He was looking at me curiously. "You do like Ashley rather a lot, don't you?"

I hesitated. I had talked with him for a few minutes beside the road when he stopped to help with the injured dog, and he had taken me out once. I could hardly claim to know much about anyone on the strength of that.

"Yes," I told Drew. "I do like him. But that proves nothing. You know," I added, "if the clothes you saw had been worn by the murderer, he could have simply wanted to get rid of them in a hurry, and dumped them somewhere around Ashley's place and Ashley found them."

Drew shook his head. "Ashley's place is a good way from where Janet was found. Anyone wanting to get rid of bloodstained clothes would hardly walk four or five hundred metres to dump them at someone's house, where they'd be found. He'd want to hide them. And Ashley wouldn't have burned them if they'd been someone else's clothes he'd found; he'd have called the police. But they were his own clothes."

"*What*?" I jumped. "Are you sure?"

"A houndstooth-check jacket and a light blue scarf.

Favourite gear of Ashley's. I've often seen him wearing them."

There was a silence while something in me shouted that this was all wrong; there had to be a mistake. Ashley Maclean, the quiet man, the gentle man, the dreamer. The man who coldly sought to kill the woman who had dropped him for another man? It didn't fit.

Suddenly and incongruously, I thought how Tony Maynard would react to the idea of Ashley Maclean committing the crime of passion. He would throw his head back and shout with laughter at the idea of Ashley doing anything so dramatic.

I felt my face flush. Did I also think Ashley was too dull to nurse such powerful emotions?

Drew interrupted my thoughts. "There's only one explanation that makes sense to me," he said. "It's not a very nice thought, because it would mean the person who killed Janet is a particularly nasty piece of goods."

"A murderer usually is, I would have thought."

"Well – yes, but even so, there are murderers and murderers, aren't there? I mean, if he hit Janet if a fit of rage in the course of an argument – sure, he's nasty. But if he arranged to meet her for the express purpose of killing her, and pinched Ashley's clothes to incriminate him, he's a good deal nastier, isn't he?"

We were sitting so still a magpie – so different from the long-tailed English magpies I knew – walked unconcernedly along the gravel path at our feet. I could hear bees busy in the azalea blooms, and the sun was warm on my back. Drew and I must have looked a perfect picture of tranquillity as we sat there and discussed the evil that lay somewhere unperceived in all this beauty.

"Pinched Ashley's clothes," I echoed. "You – you think that's what happened?"

"It's the only explanation, unless Ashley's guilty."

"But – if the murderer wanted to incriminate Ashley, why take the clothes back to the house where Ashley himself would be the most likely person to find them? Why not leave them at the scene, where the police would find them?"

"No point in doing that. It would look too much like a deliberate plant, because Ashley would never have shed his clothes on the spot if he'd been the murderer. And maybe the killer didn't care too much about incriminating Ashley. He just didn't want his own clothes to get bloodstained, maybe, and reckoned Ashley was a likely suspect. So he used the clothes and left the rest up to chance. After all, he may have left them where the chances were that only someone searching for clues would find them – and the police were likely to have a look around. They did here."

I nodded, considering. "Yes," I said. "Something like that could have happened. But if it did, it means the killer was a local person, someone who knew Ashley Maclean, knew about his friendship with Janet; and had the opportunity to get into his house."

"Oh, getting into the house and getting the clothes would be easy enough. In a quiet area like this most people never lock their houses by day as long as they're somewhere around. All anyone would have to do was make sure Ashley was out in the orchard, and the cleaning lady was hanging out clothes or something, and the rest would be easy."

"And it means the theory of the passing thug bent on robbery no longer holds water."

"Not if my guessing is anywhere near right. And Anne," he added grimly, seeming suddenly much older than his years, "if my theory is so much nonsense, which it could well be, then all the hoping in the world won't make Ashley innocent."

I looked at him for a moment. "Drew," I said slowly, "is there something else?"

He jumped. "Something else? What do you mean?"

"I just had a curious feeling that you knew something more than you've told me."

"Good God!" he snapped. "Isn't that enough?"

"Yes," I said. But I still wondered.

We sat for a long time without speaking. I could have no idea what Drew's thoughts were; but for my own part I was deeply disturbed. Not only because the evidence against Ashley was so condemning, but because now I could no longer regard myself as remote from the tragedy, as I had before. Someone within the community was a killer. What Drew had seen virtually proved that. And that meant that everyone who lived here was suspect. Certainly the person might be a stranger to me; but it was equally possible that it was someone I knew.

And I found that in spite of his swift denial I was still left with the impression that Drew knew something more about Ashley than he was prepared to tell me. I felt that although he had put forward the story of Janet dropping Ashley for a man with more money, Drew somehow knew that the story – though locally accepted as the reason for the end of the friendship – was not true. Or at least was not the whole truth.

The magpies had gone. The only sound was that of a tractor: Tony was busy somewhere among the blossoming trees; or perhaps it was Harry Gootch.

I raised my head and looked at Drew, suddenly reminded of another puzzle.

"Drew, Mrs Maynard spoke this morning about Tony coming here 'in sad circumstances'. She seemed to think I should know what she meant, but I didn't. Do you?"

He looked at me in surprise. "Why, sure. Hasn't anyone told you? It caused a big enough stir at the time."

He was obviously pleased to have a change of subject. "You see, Tony and his friend bought a second-hand car in Sydney and drove down to Melbourne and took the ferry across to Devonport and then –"

"Wait a minute," I interrupted. "Tony and his friend? What friend?"

"Oh, didn't you even know about him? I can't think what the local gossips have been about?"

"Well," I retorted, "I haven't had all that much

opportunity to pick up local gossip. I *work* here, young man; kindly remember."

He stood up with an elaborately posed look of concern. "Of course, of course! You *work* here. You're anxious to get back to your onerous duties. I mustn't delay you with further tales of drama."

He made as if to walk away and I reached out and caught the back of his sweater. "'Not so fat, varlet. Sit down and behave yourself and finish your story or I'll make steak-and-kidney for dinner – which I've heard from Mrs Gootch you detest – and you'll have to eat every mouthful in order to mind your manners in front of Mrs Maynard."

He sat down and clutched his stomach, rolling his eyes in mock despair. "Heartless wench! She would resort to torture to wrest my secrets from me! Did Mrs Gootch really tell you I can't stand steak-and-kidney?" he asked curiously.

I nodded. "Warned me most emphatically against serving it. She seems to actually *like* you, poor misguided woman. Anyway, you were safe enough. I don't like it, either."

We grinned at each other companionably.

"All right," I said. "Begin again. What friend of Tony's?"

"The chap he came out from England with. They were both coming here to Fairfield Orchard, down the east coast. I don't know why they were pushing along by driving by night, but they were. Tony was driving, and just a bit south of Swansea they met a car coming around a bend on the wrong side of the road, and Tony swerved to avoid collision. The road there runs high above the sea, but in the dark he didn't realize that they were on the edge of an almost-sheer drop, and the car went over the side. Anyway, it was either that or a head-on crash, I guess.

"The car must have rolled over and over quite a few times before it ended up among rocks. Tony says he remembers yelling: 'Jump!' and trying to undo his seat-belt when he realized the car was toppling over the edge of the drop. Then he doesn't remember what happened, except that he was standing beside the car, trying to get the passenger-side front door open, and the car was on fire. He must have been thrown out on the way down, or he'd almost certainly have been killed, or too badly hurt to do what he did. He couldn't get the door open, and the flames drove him back."

Drew paused, looking at his hands as if he realized how agonizingly frustrating the situation would be.

"They said," he went on after a moment, "that it wouldn't have made any difference if he had been able to get his mate out – he was dead, anyway. But Tony wouldn't know that at the time. I guess it was pretty rough. He burned his hands, and some of his hair was singed off, and he was generally pretty bruised and battered and had a crack on the head.

"He wasn't found till daylight, when he managed to crawl back up to the road and a passing motorist saw him, only half conscious. The car that pushed them over didn't stop – probably the driver didn't even realize he'd caused an accident. And anyone else who saw the fire evidently thought there was some harmless explanation for it. Tony was in severe shock when he was found, and couldn't remember anything for a couple of days – not even his name, nor what happened, nor where he was going. He never remembered how he spent the night, after he'd been forced to give up trying to rescue his friend – never remembered climbing back up to the road."

I sat staring at Drew until he grew impatient waiting for me to comment.

"So," he said, "that's what Mrs Maynard meant when she said Tony had arrived in sad circumstances."

"Yes," I said numbly. "I see."

But Tony hadn't arrived at all. And never would. The interloper was safe in that, at least.

"I suppose," I said slowly, "all their personal papers

were destroyed in the fire?"

Drew shrugged. "I don't know. I guess everything was destroyed except what Tony was carrying. Why?"

Then, before I could grope for an answer, he added, "Well, come to think of it, Tony must have had something on him that identified him, because they knew who he was before he got his senses back and could tell them anything, even his name. That's right, I believe it was a letter from Mrs Maynard they found in his wallet or somewhere, because the police contacted her straight away when Tony was taken to hospital."

"What," I asked, "was his friend's name?"

Drew thought for a moment. "Johnson? No. Harris – Harrison. That's it. Bob Harrison. He and Tony were friends in England – worked together, I think – they were both motor-mechanics. They'd come out to try their luck in a new country, and Tony decided to come and visit his grandmother first, before they settled down to try for work."

"Had Tony told his grandmother he and his friend were coming?"

Drew shook his head. "No. Tony said he wanted to keep it as a surprise. Not such a pleasant one as he'd planned, as it turned out."

"I should think it must have given her a pretty bad shock, with her heart condition," I suggested.

"Well, yes, I guess it did. But of course she didn't know him, then. He was her grandson, sure, but really he was a stranger. I mean, it would be a far worse knock to her now to think he'd been hurt than it was then. Anyway, he wasn't dangerously ill, or anything, though they didn't know that straight away. I guess it did shake her a bit. They brought him down to hospital in Hobart and Mrs Maynard came to stay with us so she'd be handy to the hospital to go and visit him."

He jumped up. "Gosh, I'd better go and give Tony a hand instead of discussing his near-demise. I only came in to get a splinter out, and I've been gone long enough to have an amputation."

I watched him hurry cheerfully off and my mind was racing.

At least, almost certainly, I now knew who the imposter really was. And perhaps I had some kind of explanation for the masquerade.

It was quite possible that Tony – the real Tony Maynard – in fact had been coming here in the hope of ingratiating himself with his grandmother – my grandmother – in the hope of inheriting, if not her entire estate, at least a sizeable portion of it. To an out-of-work motor-mechanic the idea of becoming the owner of a large and prosperous orchard could seem highly appealing. And that approach, certainly, would fit the cousin I had known at eighteen: Tony the opportunist.

It fitted him very well. Much better than the image of the dutiful young man looking up his lonely grandparent.

He may very well have offered his friend the chance of a steady job, or even an eventual partnership if Tony inherited the orchard – as certainly he would have had every reason to expect he would, if he could manage to make himself invaluable or even simply appealing in personality.

When Bob Harrison had regained his senses in hospital and found everyone assumed *he* was Tony Maynard, and there was no one to say he was not, he no doubt had decided to chance his arm and try to take Tony's place. That was the kind of person, I reflected, that Tony Maynard may well have chosen for a friend. And the man who now called himself Tony had the personality of a man who loved excitement and would take a gamble. And he had just the strength of character to carry it off.

I kept coming back to the fact that the Tony Maynard I had known had not seemed to me the type of fellow who would ever be keen to own an orchard. True, certainly he may have changed with the years which brought maturity.

But when I knew him he had been none too enthusiastic about work. I thought now, as I often had before, that this intruder into our family had tackled the task of learning to run an orchard with far greater enthusiasm and efficiency than Tony would have been likely to display. And, I had to admit grudgingly – as also I had done before – that he was more considerate toward Margaret Maynard than her own grandson was ever likely to have been.

Of the two men, Bob Harrison must undoubtedly have been the stronger personality. And the more attractively interesting.

I dismissed that thought, annoyed with myself for thinking it.

Of course, I thought suddenly as I stood up to go back into the house, there was one perfectly good reason for Tony to want to own Fairfield. He could sell it. An orchard of this size must really be quite valuable. I must ask someone, tactfully, what its approximate market value would be. Ashley Maclean would know.

At once the memory of the ugly thing that had happened almost at the gates of Fairfield rushed back to swamp me, and abruptly I felt weary.

I could never look at Ashley again without remembering that he very well may be a murderer. I could never look at any of our neighbours without remembering all were suspects.

Five

It was Margaret Maynard herself who gave me the first inkling of what Fairfield may be worth.

I was dusting in the living room while she was sitting in one of the easy chairs reading a book I had brought her from the public library. An easy, comfortably companionable relationship had grown up between us and we often shared good discussions on many subjects. We had much in common, though she had some very strong and sometimes unreasonable views. At first I had always carefully avoided arguments but I had gradually learned, as spring lengthened into summer, that she loved an argument and, far from being upset, thrived on it; and bore no malice toward me for thinking differently.

I paused a moment at the window to look down toward the Channel, across the orchard where the froth of pink and white blossom had given way to green foliage and tiny young fruit not yet obvious among the leaves. The scene never failed to delight me.

"You like it, don't you, Anne?" Mrs Maynard asked softly.

I turned. She had raised her head from her book and was watching me with a pleased smile.

I nodded. "I don't think anyone could fail to love Fairfield, Mrs Maynard."

I turned back to the window and said idly, "Really, being quite reasonably close to the city, and with such lovely vistas from almost every point, the orchard could become a very desirable piece of residential land, I should imagine."

Nothing had prepared me for her reaction.

There was a little pause, and then she said in a voice as sharp and brittle as broken glass: "Who put you up to raising that subject, may I ask? Was it Tony? Or has that man Renfrew been around persuading you to try to soften my attitude?"

I swung around to stare at her. Her face was white and her eyes hard with anger.

"Well?" she snapped.

"No one put me up to it," I protested. "It was simply a thought that came into my mind."

"Then you had better put it out of your mind, and keep it out! Your position here does not entitle you to interfere in my business affairs and I would be pleased if you will remember that."

"But Mrs Maynard, nothing was farther from my mind than trying to interfere in your business affairs!" There was a flick of anger in my own voice as I felt indignation rise in me at such an unfair interpretation of a casual comment. "It was an idle thought that occurred to me, and nothing more."

"Then it is an idle thought that has been occurring to rather too many people. This property is an orchard. It was tended and sweated over by my husband, and his father before him. When I was younger I worked actively on it myself, especially in the fruit season, for many years. I have picked apples early in the morning when the frost was still on them and my fingers were so numb I could scarcely grip the fruit firmly enough to pull it. I've packed them into the pine cases that were always used until these cardboard cartons came into fashion, working late into the night after the children were put to bed. And I tell you now that there is no better scent on this earth than the smell of pine boxes and tree-ripened apples. None.

"Fairfield is not for sale. It will never be for sale to some greedy businessman who will tear out the trees – trees that have borne fruit for so many years, replacing the trees that stood there before them. Trees that have been pruned with skill and sprayed with care and watched with hope. All ripped out by great vile-smelling bulldozers, and piled to die, and burned. Never!"

She struck her hand on the arm of her chair, her eyes bright with anger. "Never while there is breath in my body!"

Suddenly she gasped, stiffened as if in pain, and fell back, breathing quickly and heavily. I leapt to her chair and knelt down beside her. I knew she kept her heart-tablets always on her person, and I fumbled hastily in the pocket of her skirt, found the bottle and placed one tablet under her tongue. I closed my fingers over her wrist and felt the excited flutter of her pulse, but I had no way of knowing how dangerous this attack was. After a few moments the severity seemed to lessen, and I began to talk in a soothing tone.

"Please, Grandmother," I said gently. "Don't distress yourself. No-one has spoken to me about any possibility of selling the orchard. It was a casual remark of mine, nothing more. I can understand how you feel. I don't think I could bear to have Fairfield destroyed either, if it were mine. Certainly not if I'd known it as long as you have."

I went on holding her hand, watching her face as she lay back in the chair exhaustedly, her eyes closed, her face ashen. Presently her breathing steadied and some colour came back to her lips.

After a minute her eyes opened and met mine, piercingly blue.

"You called me Grandmother," she said.

I jumped. "Did I? Good Lord, it must have come from hearing Tony call you that. I beg your pardon."

"Don't use the Lord's name lightly in front of me," she said tartly, though her voice was still faint.

I smiled, relieved: she was feeling better. "I'm sorry, Mrs Maynard. I didn't mean any irreverence by it."

"It seems to me, young lady, that you say a good many things you don't mean. It's a bad habit."

I made to withdraw my hand and stand up, but her fingers closed suddenly over mine with surprising strength.

"I'm sorry I lost my temper, my dear. But so often in recent times – since I became ill – I've had pressure put on me – oh, very persuasively – to sell the property for development. Not only as a residential area, but as some kind of rural tourist-resort. A Singapore businessman came to Tasmania, it appears, with something like this in mind."

She made a tired gesture and went on, speaking slowly. "I don't really understand why, but there it is. He saw this place, and wanted it – oh, over three years ago, I suppose. Apparently it was exactly what he fancied, and he has never given up trying to get it, though I met the man only once. He offered a very good price. Oh, yes. And he has increased it. But I'm a traditionalist, I suppose. To destroy Fairfield just for money would be, to me, a breach of faith. A breach of faith with my husband, who loved this place; a breach of faith with his family before him, and – before *them* – the people who originally cleared and planted the land. No doubt the sweat of many a wretchedly-treated convict went into this soil. Those tragic men, too, helped create a beautiful thing. I will not have it destroyed."

I knew she shouldn't really be talking, but she seemed quite relaxed now, and I felt I might never get quite the same opportunity to ask these questions again.

"Does Tony know about the offer to buy the orchard?" I asked, half expecting to be told again that I was interfering in her business affairs. "What does he feel about it?"

Mrs Maynard smiled. "At first Tony thought I should sell. But that was before he learned how to run the orchard himself – before he found out what it means to be claimed by an affinity with the land."

"Has he been?" I asked. "Claimed by an affinity with the land?"

She looked at me, still smiling. "Wouldn't you say he had, by the way he works?"

I said carefully, "It would seem so."

"It's not so surprising. A love of the land is in his blood, after all, for all some people may scoff at such a thing."

I said nothing.

"Besides, he knows now that the orchard represents a good living, and a satisfying way of life. Once you've found a satisfying way of life, it's very foolish to change, because it's something money can't always buy."

She shook her head. "Tony no longer has any wish to sell Fairfield, I'm quite sure. Now, my dear," she added, releasing my hand, "I am quite all right, but I should like to rest for a while."

As I reached the door she said, "Anne." I paused. She

was looking at me curiously. "Tony never calls me Grandmother. He always calls me Grandma. Or Gran."

I went through to the kitchen and stood by the window for a time, forgetting the dusting. I was shaken by my slip of the tongue. I was dreadfully shaken by the spasm which had struck Mrs Maynard. And I had much to think about concerning Tony's reason for coming here, and his friend's reason for being eager to step into Tony's place. If it was three years since the first offer to buy the orchard had been made, then very probably she would have mentioned it to Tony in a letter. I wondered again how much the orchard would be worth. Considerably more to a wealthy businessman who saw it as a suitable tourist enterprise than it would be to anyone simply looking for an orchard, obviously.

The telephone interrupted my thoughts.

I answered it absently on the kitchen extension, and was jolted back to reality by the sound of Ashley Maclean's voice.

"Two things, Anne," he said pleasantly and without preamble. "First, the owner of the dog you rescued was passing yesterday and brought the dog in to show me that he'd make a perfect recovery."

I said warmly: "How nice of him! But *I* didn't rescue the dog – you did all the work."

"Well, I wouldn't have seen it but for you. Anyway, I thought you'd like to know. The second thing is, I wondered if you'd let me take you to dinner in Hobart tomorrow night. It would give me much pleasure if you would."

My fingers jerked tight on the telephone handset. The thoughtfulness, the courtesy that I had liked in Ashley Maclean were warm in his voice. But cutting across them was a mental picture of him standing with bloodstained clothes in his hands while the young woman with whom he had been friendly and who had rejected him, lay dead a few hundred metres away. How could I be in his company and not betray, by my inevitably uncomfortable behaviour, the fact that I didn't trust him?

"Anne?" he asked, puzzled.

"I – why, thank you. I'd like to do that," I heard myself say, and silently cursed myself for being such a fool.

"Fine. What time would be convenient for me to come for you? I realize you still have to prepare dinner for Mrs Maynard and Tony."

Idiot! I told myself: why didn't you think of that as an excuse for not going out with him?

We arranged a time and I hung up. After all, I reflected, the man was hardly likely to harm *me*. But I found the palms of my hands were sweating, and I had the distinct feeling I was going to have a singularly unhappy evening that would demand I call on any latent acting talents I might have, in order to pass it off. The one rewarding aspect was the fact that Ashley might be the one person I could ask about the value of Fairfield Orchard. It seemed important to know how big a prize the man who called himself Tony Maynard was gambling for.

I went back into the living room to see how Mrs Maynard was. She had fallen asleep, lying back in the big chair, her breathing easy and regular. I hesitated a moment, and then decided I knew too little of this sort of thing to take chances. I went back to the kitchen phone and called her doctor in Hobart to explain her symptoms and my ignorance of their significance.

"Everything you did was correct, Miss Baker," he reassured me. "Mrs Maynard has these attacks fairly often, sometimes she has much more severe ones which need urgent hospitalization. For this time, simply let her rest quietly."

He hesitated, and then said, "Her heart condition is unstable. I think perhaps you should know that some day one of these attacks will kill her. She knows it and I know it. It's quite unpredictable. She could live for several years, or she could die in five minutes. Beyond what you did this morning, there is nothing you *could* do. Should an attack be fatal, never blame yourself."

I put the receiver down slowly. Never blame yourself. But I had, however unwittingly, brought up the subject which so agitated her it had brought on this attack.

I went back to my work in a thoughtful frame of mind.

Tony looked sardonically amused when I told him I was going out with Ashley.

"Exciting things keep happening to you all the time, don't they?" he said mockingly. "Where's he taking you? Wrest Point?"

"The casino? I shouldn't think so."

"No," he agreed, still watching me with a smile. "I don't see Ashley as a gambling type. You should go, though. See a bit of the gay life. I'll take you myself, one evening."

He walked out without waiting to hear my answer. It was typical, I thought with a flash of anger, that Tony simply took it for granted that I'd be willing to go out with him. I presumed that with looks like his he'd gone through all his adult life assuming that any girl would be flattered to be seen out with him. It annoyed me even more because his assumption no doubt was usually correct.

As it turned out, my evening with Ashley was entirely comfortable after the first ten minutes. He was so perfectly normal, so easy to talk to, that any thought that he could resort to violence seemed so beyond reason that it scarcely entered my mind – perhaps partly because I was preoccupied by the question of the value of Fairfield Orchard.

Because behind that question hung a shadowy threat I hadn't yet consciously faced, although I knew it was there: if the prize was big enough, what might Tony Maynard's impersonator do to gain it? I had known little enough about my cousin. I knew nothing whatever of the man who had stepped into his place.

Ashley had chosen a very pleasant restaurant and we found much to talk about. He had looked at me with a smile as we went into the restaurant and said, "I promise not to deliver a history and philosophy lecture the way I did last time I took you out. To begin with, I'm not qualified to, of course. But the unqualified are usually the worst offenders at that sort of thing."

"I assure you I was interested. Really. I hope to learn a great deal more about Tasmania's history. And see a lot more of the countryside. I haven't even been to the top of Mt Wellington yet."

"Haven't you?" He looked astounded. "I thought that was the first thing everyone did when they came to Hobart – drove to the top of Mt Wellington. Or of course a visit to the casino could take top priority, depending on personal choice."

"I think I'd prefer Mt Wellington. Have you ever been to the casino?"

"A couple of times. Once Lesleigh wanted me to take her. And the first time I was driven by curiosity. It was Australia's only casino then, so it gave one a bit of dashing feeling to go, I suppose."

"Tony said he'd take me," I said half musingly.

Ashley looked at me sharply. "Did he?" He added rather quickly, "I suppose you've been to casinos in England – or maybe on the Continent?"

"I've been in Monte Carlo. They frighten me a little – the people playing, I mean. Not the ones like me, who were just there for the fun of saying they'd played the tables at Monte, even though we hadn't much idea of the difference between roulette and baccarat. The frightening part is the ones who are hooked – as much addicted to gambling as a junkie is addicted to heroin. Do you know," I added, "whether Tony often goes to the casino?"

Ashley shook his head. "I haven't any idea. Why? Do you think *he* might be a compulsive gambler?"

I remembered that I wasn't supposed to take any more

interest in Tony's behaviour than any employee would take, and I managed a quick laugh. "Oh, I shouldn't think so. He really doesn't go out very often, so he certainly doesn't play the tables regularly."

Ashley looked at me with his slow mile. "So you'd rather drive to the top of Mt Wellington than try your luck at Wrest Point? Well, it's a beautiful night, with the air as clear as the proverbial crystal. Will you let me drive you up after dinner? The lights of the city are rather lovely from the top, and the moon's full, so you'd be able to see the river."

I had smiled and said I'd enjoy it before I even remembered that Drew Thomas and I shared a terrible secret about Ashley Maclean. I promptly shut my mind against the thought. Whoever had killed Janet Chisholm had had a reason for doing it, however little any reason could justify murder. And Ashley had no reason whatever to harm me. And I was not going to think about it tonight.

The night air was mild with early summer as we left the restaurant. "It'll be much colder up on top," Ashley said, nodding toward the dark bulk of the blunt-topped mountain that lay behind the city, just discernible beyond the glow of urban lights, making me think momentarily of a drowsing dog keeping guard over its master.

The city was quickly left behind and the road began to snake its way upward in an easy gradient and the car's headlights showed the trees and bush by the roadside changing with the altitude, in the way of all mountains, and Ashley identified some of the trees for me – messmate stringybark and a shrubbery of dogwood about half-way to the twelve-hundred-metre summit giving way to urn gums and snow gums and other names strange to me. There were many dead trunks of trees, still standing, ghostly in the moonlight.

"The legacy of bushfires," Ashley explained. "The mountain's been swept by fire many times. We had disastrous fires some years ago – one great spreading horror that grew on wind and heat from a quite innocuous sort of beginning and left much of our part of the island in ruins."

"I remember," I said.

"You remember?" He looked startled. "You must have been quite young. And on the other side of the world."

I laughed. "Not that young. There was quite a lot about it in our news at the time, and I suppose I took special notice because –" I stopped hastily, carelessness having almost trapped me into saying: because I knew my grandmother lived here somewhere.

"Well," I finished, "I was young and impressionable, I suppose. Anyway, I remember. It cost a lot of lives, didn't it?"

He nodded. "Yes. It cost a lot of lives. Far too many."

His face in the reflected light from the dashboard was haunted for a moment with dark memories. Then the car rounded yet another curve in the road and the headlights showed a small animal sitting bolt upright in the middle of the road.

Ashley slammed on the brakes and stopped a couple of metres from it. My first thought – that it was a cat – was clearly wrong. This was an animal I'd never seen before: tubby and chocolate-brown, with short legs and a pink nose and fluffy tail, it sat on its hind legs, fore-paws dangling, and blinked uncomfortably in the brightness of the lights.

"Hey, old chap," Ashley said, "you'd better hop out of there! The next car along mightn't stop for you."

"What is it?" I asked.

He looked at me in astonishment and then laughed. "Sorry. I forgot for a moment you're English. It's a possum – one of our marsupial night-life-lovers. They live in the gum-trees – eat the leaves by night and sleep in hollow limbs by day."

The possum came down on all fours and scurried across the road and out of sight.

"He's lovely!" I said delightedly.

Ashley smiled and engaged the gears. "Not every fruit-grower would agree with you. They do enjoy a fruit meal in the season. I like them, though, and never begrudge them a few apples."

The road levelled out at the top in a parking area where two or three other cars were parked. We got out and stood partly sheltered by a dolomite outcrop and looked down from the splendid vantage point to the lights of Hobart, like so many glow-worms, glittering along the Derwent estuary. The cross-river bridge showed as a bar of light across the twisting ribbon of darkness that was the river.

"Didn't I read of some kind of disaster involving the bridge, once?" I asked.

"You seem to have taken an interest in Tasmanian affairs," Ashley commented. "Yes, I'm afraid you're right. A ship struck one of the bridge pylons and smashed it and a section of the bridge collapsed. It was night and when the span fell the bridge lights went out, and there was traffic on the bridge, naturally, and the drivers had no way of knowing what had happened. Several cars simply drove into space, and two had incredible escapes – were left hanging over the broken span. A number of people died."

He turned to glance at me in the moonlight. "I seem to be talking nothing but disasters tonight, but you did ask. Let's switch to Geography."

He pointed out the various areas of the city, from the wharves to Risdon across the river where Lieutenant Bowen had first been sent to found the European settlement of Tasmania with a somewhat ill-assorted collection of human beings.

Presently Ashley gave a little laugh. "Anne, you must be frozen, and I go rambling on like an over-talkative tourist guide. Let's go back."

He helped me into the car and went around to slip in under the wheel. "You're very quiet. I'm afraid I've been boring company."

I shook my head quickly. "No. But – well, speaking of the accident to the bridge made me think of the accident when Tony and his friend were on their way to Fairfield. And that led me to think of the orchard itself. Mrs Maynard told me yesterday that some Chinese businessman wanted to buy it to turn it into a tourist complex. She was very upset."

"Has Renfrew approached her again?"

"I don't think so. She mentioned that name, though – Renfrew. Who is he?"

"A real-estate agent who acts as representative for the consortium who want to buy the orchard. A Mr Quong Lee Heng is apparently the head of the group of wealthy Singapore businessmen who want to launch out into the tourist business in Australia and think Tasmania is an ideal spot to promote."

"But why choose Fairfield?"

He shrugged and started the car. "It just appealed to Mr Quong, I guess, and I get the impression he's the kind of man who is accustomed to getting what he wants. After all, it's a lovely spot. And it's fairly centrally situated to most of the places that could have the greatest appeal to tourists – handy to Hobart, and so to the major airport, and our old friend the casino. Day tours to places like Port Arthur, with historical significance, and plenty of scenic areas would be very important to an organization offering a package-holiday deal, which presumably Mr Quong's syndicate would be doing. Oh, yes, I think it probably makes sense, if you have the kind of money Mr Quong and his friends evidently have to spend."

"So Fairfield would be a prettily-located hotel? Why buy a whole orchard for that?"

"Oh, I think it'd be much more than just a hotel. A luxury hotel, certainly. But a whole complex, I gather – including a working orchard displayed for the tourist, as I understand it. Plus a park, golf, tennis, riding, saunas and all the rest. And not only for Asians, of course. The set-up would be designed to appeal to Australian tourists also – especially mainland tourists. That's as Mr Quong outlined his plans to Mrs Maynard."

I said slowly, "She hates the idea. Passionately. I was

really quite frightened by her agitation yesterday when a casual remark of mine brought the subject up. I was terrified she might have a severe heart attack."

He nodded, his eyes on the road as it wound its way downward.

"I know. She had always made her opinions of any such sale very clear. And yet, in spite of it, she might have been forced by her ill-health to sell, if Tony hadn't come. Though I doubt if she would have sold. She'd have engaged a manager, or leased it to someone, rather than have it changed."

"But if the Chinese were going to keep the orchard functioning –"

"Only a small fragment of it, and not as a genuine orchard. Just a – a sort of model orchard – as a display to show how trees are tended and fruit is picked – a fun thing, no more. She hated the whole idea. I think she'd rather have seen Fairfield fall into decay through a succession of bad managers than taken over by hordes of tourists. No matter how handsome a sum they offered."

"Do you have any idea how much the orchard would be worth? To Mr Quong's syndicate?"

I wondered if he would think my curiosity a bit too presumptuous in a housekeeper-companion, but he answered readily.

"The original sum Mr Quong offered was half a million dollars. I know he has since raised it, but to what figure I don't know, but I suspect around three quarters of a million."

I sat in numbed silence. Three quarters of a million dollars. An attractive prize indeed.

Tony Maynard would have known about it before he left England; there could be little doubt of that. Mrs Maynard had told me more than once that she had often written to Tony, telling him of orchard affairs, even though he only sent her a post-card about once a year. He was the only relative whose address she knew, so she kept on writing to him because one needed someone in the family to talk to, even if it was very largely a one-way conversation, she said.

And if Tony had known, so had his friend, who now lived at Fairfield as the obvious heir.

"That," I said eventually, realizing Ashley would be expecting me to comment, "is a sizeable fortune."

He nodded. "But to someone like Mrs Maynard, a fortune isn't very important. The orchard more than caters for all her wants. At her time of life and in her state of health, what would she want with a huge sum of money?"

I glanced at him. "What about your property? How would you feel about selling it? I mean, it adjoins Fairfield – surely it must be in the running for Mr Quong's attention, too?"

He laughed and shook his head. "Mrs Maynard thinks I'm lovely because I haven't any plans to sell my orchard, either, but in fact it really isn't worth a cracker to Mr Quong. It doesn't have Fairfield's wonderful and extensive views, and that's what makes Fairfield so appealing as a tourist resort."

"Does your orchard have a name?"

"Oakhill. The original owner of Fairfield took up enough land to make the two properties, and he gave the smaller to his son. He must have liked English oaks. There are a dozen fair-sized trees at various points on my place."

"May I come and see it some time?"

"Of course. Please do. The house is very attractive – perhaps as attractive as Fairfield, though smaller. But I did warn you the views are not so spectacular, though I like them."

He drove in silence for a minute and then added, "In a way, I suppose I do share Mrs Maynard's feelings. It would be sad to see an orchard like Fairfield destroyed. So much human endeavour has gone into it over the generations. But to be honest I have to admit I'm not sure whether I'd have the strength of my convictions if my property were as valuable as hers."

His face and voice were suddenly hard. "But that might be because too high a price has been paid for my property already."

We were down off the mountain and without warning he put his foot down, hurling the car too fast through the night, his hands firm on the wheel, his eyes bright with bitterness as he seemed to concentrate his whole being on driving – and driving with great skill – as if he wanted to shut some demon out of his mind.

Dumbfounded, I sat back in the seat and watched the road, and hoped desperately that his full concentration *was* on the car. I had no idea what he had meant by paying 'too high a price' for his property, and I didn't dare ask. Whatever it was, it was some cruel thing which turned him from a gentle, considerate man who drove moderately and intelligently into a madman who challenged death – and, I felt, was perfectly prepared to lose. And yet he drove brilliantly.

We had travelled perhaps twenty kilometres before he slowly eased the speed back. Presently he glanced sidways at me. "I'm sorry," he said, "I wasn't listening. Did you say something?"

He seemed quite unaware of how long the silence had been, and the black mood had passed, or been suppressed.

I swallowed hard. "Mrs Maynard believes Tony shares her love for Fairfield," I said, trying to carry on the conversation as if there had scarcely been a break. "And her conviction it shouldn't be sold."

Ashley laughed. "He'd be both ends and the middle of a fool if he didn't persuade the old lady that those were his sentiments. Grandson or not, he'd stand precious little chance of inheriting the orchard if Mrs Maynard suspected that as soon as she was buried he'd be selling it up for a hotel site."

I looked at him keenly for a moment. It was as if whatever tormented him had been left behind, at least for the time being – outpaced by that brief, wild drive.

He was a good friend of Mrs Maynard's; it was quite possible she had taken him into her confidence over her plans. "*Will* Tony inherit?" I asked.

"Oh, yes. Mrs Maynard told me she was leaving him Fairfield. After all, he's her grandson, her only relative."

"She has a granddaughter, too," I protested, and added hastily, "she told me that."

Ashley nodded. "Yes, I believe she has. I'd forgotten. But after all, it's a granddaughter she's never seen, and with whom she's never had contact, and whose whereabouts on the other side of the world she doesn't know. The granddaughter can hardly weigh very heavily against Tony's presence and hard work. And his devotion to Mrs Maynard. No doubt the girl will get something, but I rather fancy she'll have to be content with a relatively small cash legacy. Anyway, she probably has a husband to look after her."

He turned into the driveway of Fairfied and added, "Even Drew Thomas will have to be content with a comparatively minor legacy now."

"Drew?" I queried quickly. "But Drew isn't a relative. Is he?"

"No, but he's been like a grandson to Mrs Maynard all his life, and you must remember Tony only appeared on the scene two years ago. Up until then, he hadn't meant much more to her than her granddaughter means now. On the other hand, Drew has always been someone special to her, ever since he was little."

"Are you saying you think Drew might have inherited Fairfield, if Tony hadn't turned up?"

"Yes. I know he would have, because some years ago Mrs Maynard asked me to be one of the witnesses to her will, and she told me she had left Drew Fairfield Orchard. There were quite solid cash legacies to both her grandchildren, but they would have been minor compared with the value of Fairfield."

I said slowly, "Drew hasn't much occasion to be kindly

disposed toward Tony, then."

"Oh, Drew never knew he'd been named as heir to Fairfield. I'm sure such a thought would never have crossed his mind. Even his parents knew nothing of it, so Mrs Maynard said. In fact, she was adamant that they shouldn't know, and I'm afraid I certainly had no right to tell you."

"It's all right," I assured him quickly. "They won't hear of it from me."

He smiled and nodded.

"I hope," I said musingly, "that Drew is given a substantial legacy under Mrs Maynard's new will. After all, as you say, he's been like a grandson to Mrs Maynard all his life, and I'm sure he's genuinely fond of her."

"Oh, he is, no doubt of it. But the fact remains he's *not* her grandson."

At that moment I came very close to saying: neither is Tony. Sometimes I wonder what, in the end, would have happened if I had. Wonder whether in fact it all might have ended very differently.

Ashley added, "I'm sure Drew wouldn't be ignored, though I don't know anything about the terms of Mrs Maynard's new will and I wasn't witness to it. I only know that she told me she was leaving Fairfield to Tony."

He got out of the car and came around to open the door for me. At the front door he stood for a moment looking down at me with a half-smile. Then he bent and kissed me as lightly and casually as if he had been my brother.

"Goodnight, Anne. Thank you for coming out with me." And he was gone, striding back to his car and driving off as I let myself into the house.

I thought how derisively Tony would have laughed. Tony, I would take a bet at very long odds, never said goodnight so casually to any girl he took out. And immediately I was angry with myself for my habit of comparing Ashley with Tony – and finding Ashley somewhat colourless in the comparison.

In my room I stood for a little while at the window, looking out at the night before switching on any light. For a moment in the car I had wanted to tell Ashley about Tony, to ease the weight of my secret by sharing it. Why hadn't I done so?

Perhaps because I was still shaken by that strange black mood that had seized him and caused him to drive through the night like a madman – and to seem almost unaware of having done it.

I had always felt Ashley was a gentle man. But now I realized there was a violence in him I didn't in the least understand. And, against my will, I though again of him standing with bloodstained clothes in his hands the morning after Janet Chisholm died.

The night air seemed suddenly chill, and I turned away from the window with a little shiver, and turned on the light as if it would somehow banish the doubts that lurked half-unheeded in my mind like ghosts skulking in shadowed corners.

Six

I was taken by surprise when Lesleigh Martin phoned me.

I hadn't seen her since the Masons' party, and although she had said then that she would arrange a game of golf with me I had assumed it was simply one of those half-invitations people so often issue on the spur of the moment: 'You must drop in and see us next time you're in town' – and no one would be more astonished if you did.

But Lesleigh's voice, crisp and businesslike, said, "What about that game of golf? Are you free for nine holes on Thursday afternoon? Good. I'll pick you up about one-thirty. Don't worry if you don't have your own clubs – you can hire a set from the club pro."

I had just taken my golf-bag out to the front door on the Thursday afternoon when I heard a car coming up the drive. I stepped out, expecting it to be Lesleigh, but it was a police car, and two detectives in neat business-suits got out. The older man looked me over with an appraising glance which made me feel he could stand up in court a month later and describe in detail and on oath exactly how I looked and what I was wearing.

"Detective Sergeant Ericson," he said briefly. "We should like to speak with Mrs Maynard, please."

I showed them into the livingroom and went to Mrs Maynard's room to tell her.

She put down the book she had been reading and sat for a moment looking down at her hands in her lap. Then she stood up and reached for her walking-stick.

"Are you sure you feel well enough to see them?" I asked.

"Of course," she said impatiently. "It's just that it still comes as something of a shock to realize that there are policemen in my house who want me to tell them something that may convict someone I know of murder."

I stared at her and she smiled. "Oh, no, my dear, I don't know any such fearful secret. If I did, I would tell them, no matter whom it might convict. Murder is not excusable, not something one covers up to oblige a friend."

I paused at the livingroom door. "Shall I stay?"

"No, of course not. I'm sure that's Lesleigh's car in the drive now. Go and enjoy your game, Anne. I shall be perfectly all right." She opened the livingroom door. "I don't think Sergeant Ericson has come to arrest me. Have you, Sergeant?"

The two men stood up. "Not today, Mrs Maynard." The sergeant smiled, and there was respect in his eyes.

"You see, Anne," Mrs Maynard said, "we have met before, the sergeant and I. A number of times."

"And I'm sorry to intrude again," the sergeant said courteously, helping her into a chair. "But there's always the possibility, you know, that there's something we've overlooked – some small detail –"

I went out to meet Lesleigh.

She was standing beside a Kelly-green Fiat X19 sports sedan and looking, in cream slacks and dark brown silk shirt, as lithe and beautiful as I remembered her. She jerked her head at the police car as I put my clubs into her car.

"Are the fuzz on about Janet Chisholm again?"

I nodded. "They wanted to see Mrs Maynard."

"Why?"

"I gather they just keep hoping someone will remember something that might provide the proverbial vital lead. Or, as Tony once put it, they keep asking the same questions to see whether they get the same answers."

Lesleigh spun the wheel and headed the car back down the drive. "They'll never find out who did it," she said. "Not now."

"Doesn't that worry you?"

She seemed to consider the question. "I guess that depends on who did it," she said presently.

"You mean you'd be prepared to see some people get away with *murder*?"

"I might. In certain circumstances. Oh, I wish the wretched girl had never come here. Let's talk about something else."

"Of course," I agreed. "But you can't just sweep murder under the carpet."

She gave a quick laugh. "Oh, make no mistake, Anne, the local people haven't swept it under the carpet just because they don't talk about it, and some of them, I guess – like me – don't really want to know. It's not a nice thought that one of your neighbours, or a friend, could be a murderer."

"Are you afraid of learning who the murderer is?"

She took a little while to answer. "I'm more afraid of the police learning who the murderer is."

I looked at her sharply. "Do you *know* –" I stopped. "I'm sorry. That's unfair. We're setting out to play golf, not hold an enquiry. I warn you I'm hardly Australian Open material at the best of times, and to add to my ineptitude I'm rather out of practice."

We talked golf the rest of the way. The course was an attractive one and I thoroughly enjoyed the nine holes we played, though Lesleigh was, as I'd expected, much the better player. However, my game didn't let me down too badly and I found Lesleigh surprisingly good company.

Back at the club-house I bought drinks and we sat at a quiet table. "Thank you for the game," I said. "I really enjoyed it, even if you did thrash me."

She gave me a little smile. "You're no mean hand with a golf-club yourself. I enjoyed it, too. One of the good things about sport is that while you're playing you've got to concentrate on it and forget everything else."

She put the glass down on the table. "Even murder."

I said, "I'm sorry I sounded like a television detective in the car. I won't drag it up again."

She shook her head. "Why shouldn't you ask questions? You live here now, and there's every likelihood one of your neighbours is a murderer. You've every right to want to know at least as much as the rest of us know. I was wrong to ask you not to talk about it."

She sipped her drink. "You wanted to ask if I knew the murderer's identity. I only know what everyone in the district knows. That Ashley Maclean is suspect number one, at least with the police. And if Ashley killed her, most people in this district don't really want to know. That's why they don't talk much about it. And that's what I meant when I said I didn't want the police to know – not if it was Ashley."

"Is he so important to you?" I asked incautiously.

She laughed. "Not the way you mean. Ashley's a bit too quiet for me. It's just that if Ashley killed her, she damned well deserved it."

"Does anyone deserve to be murdered?"

"Oh, don't moralize, Anne! I don't know what she did.

But I know that if she drove a man like Ashley Maclean to murder, she did something very rotten."

"She dropped him for another man who had more money, I've been told."

"It seemed so. But Ashley would never commit murder just for that."

I felt my stomach muscles tense as I recalled that I had believed Drew Thomas may have known another reason.

"A man like Ashley Maclean," I repeated thoughtfully. "But what sort of a man is he? Do you really know? Does anyone really know what sort of person anyone else is?"

I was remembering my wild drive through the night with Ashley, and I told Lesleigh about those few strange minutes.

Lesleigh was silent for a while, carefully making a little pattern in the frosting of water-droplets on the outside of her glass with her forefinger. "Yes," she said slowly. "It's a queer thing. You can think about people you know and say with absolute certainty that this person or that would never steal. But which person is incapable of murder, if he or she is pushed far enough? For some reason, it's not as easy to be sure. And Janet Chisholm was a bitch."

She said it in a voice as brittle and dangerous as broken glass.

"And having said that, I should apologize to all female dogs."

She glanced at me. "Janet was a parasite. I got curious to know why a qualified nurse was working as a housekeeper, so I did some checking. In my previous job as secretary to an MP, I'd had some experience at that sort of thing."

I felt a stab of uneasiness, wondering if I also rated a background study.

"Janet took jobs as a nurse, or a housekeeper, or a companion, only for elderly or terminally-ill patients. That's the pattern she followed for years. She was kind and thoughtful and made herself indispensable. You'd be surprised how often they left her a legacy. It ran up to a good total over the years. No-one lived long under Janet's tender care."

I stared. "Good God! You're not suggesting she *killed* them?"

"No. She carefully only undertook work where her employer was sure not to live long. I personally suspect she probably didn't try very hard to prolong her patients' lives, once she had what she wanted. But that's pure speculation on my nasty part. What I'm getting at is that she had few scruples. There was at least one occasion in the past when she had probably tried her hand at blackmail. It's always possible she tried it again. And a blackmailer can push his victim just too far."

"You think she tried to blackmail *Ashley*? Over what?"

She shrugged. "I haven't the least idea whether she tried to blackmail Ashley or anyone else, or on what grounds. But she was obviously good at researching people's backgrounds. Maybe she found something about someone – not necessarily Ashley, because that's presupposing he killed her, and I don't assume that."

She took a quick drink and set the glass down rather harder than necessary. "Lord, girl, I don't *know* anything. And I don't want to know. But I think I can explain what Ashley meant when he said too high a price had already been paid for his orchard, and why that memory would be enough to send him temporarily a little crazy. And it had nothing to do with Janet Chisholm."

I waited.

"You won't remember, and probably never even heard about it, but there were huge fires around this area – oh, twelve, thirteen years ago."

"I remember."

She looked at me in surprise, as Ashley had. "Good grief, do you? I thought people on the other side of the world barely noticed what happened to us."

I shrugged. "Maybe we're not as ill-informed as we seem."

"I was living in Hobart at the time, of course, not here on the orchard," she went on. "We didn't own it then, and I was still at school, and I certainly didn't know Ashley, so I only know the story as it's been told to me. Ashley has never spoken of it to me."

She finished her drink. "Ashley would have been only about eighteen or nineteen. He was a student at Hobart University, but he was at home when the fire broke out. There was a combination of heat and dry weather unusual for Tasmania, and there was a howling wind. And those, combined with a small fire which maybe didn't rate the attention it should have, were the ingredients of nightmare. In a matter of hours a great slice of the countryside was on fire and the fire moved at frightful speed, because once a wind-fanned fire really gets going it makes its own wind and you can get fire-storm – and that, on top of what was blowing before, can be really something."

She lit a cigarette.

"Ashley and his father and older brother were out helping to try to save a neighbour's place when Ashley, who was working a little way from the others, rushed up and shouted that the fire was heading for their own orchard. Mrs Maclean – his mother – was alone in the house with no motor vehicle to escape in, even if anyone had known a safe place to escape to. Ashley said at the rate the fire was travelling there'd be no time to get there by the main road. But there's a dirt track called Pattersons' Lane, and he said they might have time to get there, to the house, that way.

"Donald – Ashley's brother – and his father left the other men to continue the fight on that property, and jumped into their car and raced off toward their own orchard, and Ashley ran to his elderly Mini – the battered sort of thing a rather hard-up student might be likely to own, I gather. It refused to start, and Ashley was left behind. By the time he got it going a few minutes later, Pattersons' Lane was blocked by fire, and his father and brother were dead."

I stared at her in horror. "Oh, God," I whispered.

She nodded.

"Ashley drove home by the main road. The house was intact, his mother quite safe. The fire had just taken a corner of the orchard and then veered off and gone on its way. It was one of those freaks of fire-behaviour which occur with every outbreak. Afterwards, Ashley came home to the orchard. It was no secret that he'd always lamented the fact that the place wasn't big enough for both him and his brother. Now he had it to himself. But I dare say he didn't feel he wanted it then."

"No," I said in a shaken voice. Too high a price, indeed.

"He was sensible about it," Lesleigh said. "He accepted what fate had thrown at him, and kept the orchard and worked it, the way he'd always wanted to. I guess in time he must have come to love it again. Besides, it was his mother's home, and they say in spite of what had happened she wanted to go on living there, wanted Ashley to keep it. She didn't live there very long after that, I believe. The shock undermined her health and she went into a nursing home in Hobart. She still lives there, a semi-invalid."

"That kind of shock would be enough to damage anyone, I should think."

She stubbed out her cigarette. "I dare say. There were a good many people who were left shattered after those couple of days of fires. And a good many left dead."

We went out to the car, neither of us speaking. I was trying to grasp the enormity of the thing, the recurring horror Ashley must feel, even after all these years – a horror made so much worse by the fact that he had been the one to raise the alarm, the one to make the judgment that the fire was going to engulf the orchard and the house; the one to advise going by the short-cut that became a death-trap. Small wonder he had felt the need to vent his pent-up feelings that night when I had so unwittingly made him remember what he could not bear to remember, and could never forget.

I slid into the passenger seat of the car and as Lesleigh

got in behind the wheel she dropped her sun-glasses on the floor, and I bent and picked them up.

"Never mind, I shan't want them at this time of day," she said, starting the car and backing it out of its parking-bay.

"I'll just put them in here, then," I said, reaching out to open the glove-box.

"Leave it!" Lesleigh snapped, her hand flashing out to close over my wrist.

But she was a fraction too late and I had already opened the glove compartment. And I had seen what was in it.

Syringes in a plastic case. Hypodermic needles. Something in a bottle. And a small packet which, I instantly suspected, would if opened reveal a white powder.

I sat perfectly still, just staring. Lesleigh, I suddenly realized, had worn long sleeves, even today when it was quite hot. Why? To hide the needle-marks on her arms?

Slowly I turned my head to look at her. There was something near to hatred in the green eyes that met mine in a hard stare.

"I'm sorry," I stammered. "I didn't mean –"

She shrugged and turned her head away and shifted the gears to drive out from the parking-lot to the road.

"I always keep the bloody glove-box locked. Why I forgot today I'll never know. I'm a diabetic, Anne. I have to carry insulin with me always. But nobody knows, and nobody is going to know. Do you understand?"

"But why? There's no shame in being diabetic!" I protested.

"I said nobody is going to know." Her voice was even and quiet, and something about it was frightening. "Not even my brothers. And you will hold your tongue."

I still stared at her, certain that I had stumbled into waters where I was out of my depth.

"Of course," I said. "If that's what you want."

She said in the same icy voice, "That's what I want. And

that's what you'll do, if you don't want to end up like Janet Chisholm."

And in that moment I felt it was no empty threat. I said with a calmness I didn't in the least feel, "I'm not the gossiping kind. It's your business. It remains so."

She drove for a moment without looking at me. Then she flung me a quick, hard glance, and nodded.

After a minute she said in a perfectly ordinary tone, "I liked the way you played the seventh to avoid those devilish bunkers. For someone who'd never been on the course before, it was cunning."

"It's very similar to one of the holes on the course I learned to play on in Yorkshire," I told her, and the conversation returned to something remarkably normal.

Back at Fairfield I waved her a cheerful thanks as she drove off after we'd arranged to play again. Inside, I put my golf bag down in my room and stood quite still for a minute.

Lesleigh was lying. I was sure of it. On the two occasions I had been with her she had made no attempt to follow a diabetic's vital diet. Whatever she carried in the glove-compartment of her car, it was not insulin. I suspected it was heroin.

"Is that you, Anne?" Mrs Maynard's light, clear voice called.

"Yes." I pulled my scattered wits together and walked slowly toward her room, feeling thoroughly shaken. It was foolish, I told myself, to be so upset. I scarcely knew Lesleigh. Yet, for all her oddly blunt manner, even in the couple of hours we had spent in each other's company I had grown to like her considerably.

She was clever, witty, polished, and one of the most beautiful women I had ever seen. And she was doomed, unless I was greatly mistaken. Anyone on hard drugs was doomed. It was only a question of time, unless she sought expert help, and somehow I couldn't see her doing that.

The sadness of it, the fearful *waste*, was a hard, knotted

sensation in my throat as if I wanted to cry.

Mrs Maynard was sitting in her usual chair, leaning back against its high back as if she was weary. There was a book open on her lap, but she was looking out of the window at the orchard and pasture sweeping down to the water of the Channel. She was wearing a dress of deep jade jersey and her short, softly-waving hair was as always immaculately groomed. I reflected, as I had often done before, that she must have been a quite beautiful woman when she was young. I wondered whether the confident authority, almost arrogance, had always been part of her, or had been acquired with age.

Beside her, I always felt untidy, windblown and lacking in poise, yet she never made me feel uncomfortable.

She turned from the window and smiled at me. "Did you and Lesleigh have a nice game?"

"Thank you, yes. Can I get you something? A cup of tea?"

"No, thank you. Sit down, my dear, I want to talk to you."

I hesitated a second, thinking it was time I got dinner started, and she correctly interpreted my hesitation.

"If dinner is fifteen minutes late no-one will starve, including Tony, who must wait," she said.

I smiled and sat down in the chair facing hers.

"Anne, you have by now met various local people, and naturally many will have spoken to you about Janet's death."

I nodded. "Yes. An unsolved murder in the midst of a country community isn't easily forgotten."

"No." Percy the black cat jumped on to her lap and she stroked him absently. "Has anyone been – critical of Janet? Spoken of her as if they didn't like her?"

I hesitated a shade warily. "Yes," I said. "More than one person has given me the impression they didn't like her particularly."

She looked hard at me and I thought she was going to ask

me for names, but she looked down at Percy and said, "Strange. I liked Janet. I liked her very much, and I have always believed myself a good judge of character. Apparently I was wrong."

I waited.

She went on, "Ashley and she were good friends at one time, but something happened to end the friendship. People said it happened because Janet dropped Ashley for someone else, but it did seem to me at the time that it was Ashley who ended the association. Perhaps he saw a side to Janet's character I didn't see. You say others have given you the impression they didn't like Janet, so perhaps I was blind to something I should have seen."

I said, "Why do you think that?"

"When Sergeant Ericson was here today he asked me whether I had any idea where Janet might have been getting regular payments of money, quite apart from wages, over the last few weeks before she was killed."

I started. "*Was* she getting regular payments?"

"Quite substantial payments."

"Perhaps she had gambling wins," I suggested lamely.

Mrs Maynard smiled faintly. "The sergeant said the money was paid into her bank account in cash at precisely fortnightly intervals, and always exactly the same amount. He said it had the appearance of blackmail payments."

She shook her head a little sadly. "It doesn't seem possible, either that Janet was a blackmailer or that there should be anyone in this district with an ugly enough secret to warrant paying money to cover it up."

I was staring at her. I knew two people who might well have fallen victim to a blackmailer, if she had somehow stumbled across their secrets. I couldn't imagine how Janet could have learned about Tony, but since I had just blundered into Lesleigh Martin's secret, it was perfectly possible Janet Chisholm could have done the same thing. And Lesleigh had done some detailed checking on Janet's background, which might be regarded as a strange thing to do unless she had a real reason for it.

Mrs Maynard looked at me dubiously. "What is it, Anne? Do *you* know some reason Janet may have been blackmailing someone?"

I glanced down at my hands in my lap. "It's just that Lesleigh Martin was talking about Janet this afternoon, without very much affection. She had checked up on Janet's past – I presume because she didn't trust her and was upset over her friendship with Ashley Maclean."

Mrs Maynard nodded with a little smile. "Yes, I can see Lesleigh doing that out of loyalty to Ashley. She was very fond of him once, I understand – probably still is, though they're not particularly compatible, I think. I've only met Lesleigh a few times, but I rather think she's the type to stand by her friends."

Her face became serious. "What did she tell you about Janet?"

"That she was once suspected of having been involved in blackmail, but it was purely a suspicion."

"I see."

There was a little silence. Then I asked, "Did Sergeant Ericson say how much Janet was being paid?"

"She had banked a thousand dollars each fortnight for the last six weeks before she was killed."

"Three thousand dollars," I said thoughtfully. "So if she was blackmailing someone it wasn't a wealthy person. If it had been, she'd have demanded one very large lump sum, surely. But if a person in ordinary financial circumstances was being pressed to pay five hundred dollars a week – well, it isn't something anyone could go on doing for long, is it?"

Mrs Maynard fondled Percy's ears. "No. So if Janet was a blackmailer, there is the motive for her murder. And it means beyond doubt she was killed by a local person. Perhaps someone I know." She leaned back tiredly, her face sad. "Janet. I thought I knew her. I didn't know her at all."

I bent forward and touched her hand. "From what Lesleigh told me Janet could show a very charming face to her employer, but it was something of a mask, I'm afraid, if Lesleigh's interpretation of things in Janet's past was correct."

Mrs Maynard nodded. "That coincides with what Sergeant Ericson told me. According to him Janet was a rather unpleasant person, appearing to take jobs only where her patient wasn't likely to live long and might be influenced to leave at least a small bequest to her as an invaluable companion. And an invaluable companion she made herself in my case."

She passed a hand wearily across her face. "Such things tend to make one lose faith in humanity, which is rather foolish when it's only faith in one's own judgment which is under question."

Hurt rose in my throat at the thought of the desperate sorrow she would feel if she ever learned that she had given her trust and affection to the imposter under her roof.

"It isn't possible to pick the diamond from the imitation every time without a magnifying glass," I said. "In any case, Janet's apparent affection for you may very well have been real."

She smiled at me. "Thank you, Anne. Now I mustn't keep you any longer."

I stood up and Percy jumped off Mrs Maynard's knee and followed me, just as Butch, the black and white cat, met me at the door.

"All right, you standover merchants," I told them. "I'll give you your dinner first."

As if they understood what I'd said they scampered friskily down the passageway and as I started to follow Mrs Maynard said, "Anne."

I stopped and looked back at her.

"You said people had spoken to you without affection of Janet. Have you any idea whom she may have been blackmailing?"

"No," I said, and wondered whether I had spoken too quickly.

When Tony came in he went along to see Mrs Maynard, as he usually did after a day in the orchard. It was one of his appealing habits to not only tell her what was being done on a day-to-day basis but also to confer with her on general aspects of running the property. Harry Gootch also came at least twice a week to keep her abreast of even the most routine work being done, and often on days when she was feeling well one or other of them would drive her about the orchard and down to the sheep-pastures, or she would walk around the machinery sheds with the aid of her stick and look at everything with alert and knowledgeable eyes, and it hadn't taken me long to realize that Drew had been right when he said she kept her hand on the reins.

I guessed that certainly she would have told Tony what the police had said about Janet, but he said nothing to me when he came back.

Mrs Maynard came out to have her dinner with Tony and me, and during the meal she looked up suddenly. "Goodness, how could I have forgotten! Tony, I had the most unexpected letter in the mail today – an airmail from London."

We both looked at her.

"Anne, could I trouble you to bring me the letter? It's on my bedside table."

I went to fetch it, curiosity compelling me to look at the return address on the back of the envelope. The sender was a G. Forbes, with a Kensington address, which meant precisely nothing to me.

Mrs Maynard took the letter and opened it. "I shall read it out, and it will explain itself: 'Dear Mrs Maynard, I hope I have been given the correct address, and that you will forgive me for writing. I don't like to trouble you, but I wonder if you could give me the address of your grandson, Tony? I have been living and working in Canada for almost three years, and lost touch with Tony – he was always a bad correspondent and I'm little better – though once we were close friends.' "

I instinctively flicked a glance at Tony. He met my eye and raised one eyebrow quizzically, but otherwise his face was impassive.

Mrs Maynard continued to read.

" 'I returned to England a few months ago, but find I still have itchy feet and want to be on the move again. This time I'm planning to visit Australia, leaving in just under three weeks, and I have just learned from a mutual acquaintance that Tony migrated out there a couple of years ago and intended to visit you. Finding out your address took a little bit of sleuthing on my part, but I think I may have it right. If Tony is still in Australia and you know his present address, it would be rather nice for me to be able to contact him, as I know no-one else in that country. I do apologize for presuming to ask favours of you, but if it is not too great an inconvenience, I should be most grateful. Sincerely yours, Glenda Forbes.' "

Tony's eyes were on Mrs Maynard's face as she looked up from the letter, and he was smiling.

"Glenda!" he said delightedly. "Yes, of course, I remember she went to Canada. I'm afraid what she says about me being a rotten correspondent in quite true."

"I'm aware of it," Mrs Maynard said drily.

He made a wry face and resumed eating. "Sorry, Grandma. But I was always hopeless with a pen. Anyway, I took it for granted that Glenda had lots of diversions in Canada and wouldn't spare me a thought."

"Well, I shall certainly write to her at once and invite her to come to stay at Fairfield for a time. The letter doesn't make it clear whether she is planning to live and work in Australia or is just coming out for a holiday. What work does she do?"

"Secretarial, if I remember rightly. But she's a versatile person." He smiled. "She might like to take a temporary job here as a fruit-picker."

There wasn't a flicker of concern or alarm in his face, whatever he might be feeling. And, I reflected, he must be feeling extreme alarm. He had probably never even heard of Glenda Forbes in his life, and now this friend from Tony Maynard's past was about to descend on Fairfield and blow Bob Harrison's masquerade sky high.

All he did was grin at Mrs Maynard. "Now don't go expecting the big romantic bit, Grandma. We were pretty good friends once, Glenda and I, but that's all."

I had to admit to myself the man was a consummate actor.

How much more than that was he? I felt that Tony the adventurer, the opportunist, would not brook too much interference with his plans. Although I couldn't imagine circumstances which would have let Janet learn the truth about him, if she had done so then certainly he was a prime target for blackmail. And if Janet was a blackmailer – as her bank account so strongly suggested – then *she* had been a prime target for murder.

But murder by whom?

Because there was also Lesleigh Martin. If Janet had found Lesleigh was a drug addict, then Lesleigh also became a target for blackmail, and I had the strong impression that Lesleigh, too, could be dangerous if she found herself threatened. She had told me to hold my tongue if I didn't want to wind up murdered like Janet; and I thought the threat was not just so many empty words.

That night before I went to bed I walked out into the garden and sat on the wooden bench beside the azaleas. Their blooms were finished now, gone with the advance of summer, but it was not the beauty of the garden which was foremost in my mind. I had to do some clear thinking.

Whatever Janet Chisholm had been in life, she had been murdered, and her murderer went free.

I knew two people – presumably not seriously considered as suspects by the police – who *may* have been blackmail victims. It did not necessarily follow that either of them had killed Janet even if she had been preying on them. And neither Lesleigh nor Tony was necessarily the person who had made fortnightly payments of a thousand dollars to Janet.

The police, of course, could check in a flash whether either Lesleigh or Tony had been withdrawing that sort of money from their bank accounts. It was surely my duty to go to the police and tell them what I knew.

Yet if I did, I berayed Lesleigh Martin. Or was there a chance her addiction could be cured, if an arrest and probably imprisonment for drug possession forced her separation from whichever of the hard drugs she was using?

I ran my fingers through my hair, deeply troubled. Lesleigh was highly intelligent. If there was a real chance of cure, surely would take it herself? Did I have any right to make that kind of decision for her?

And if I told the police about Tony –

No. I had made my decision there months ago, and nothing had happened to make me change my mind. Exposing Tony would have to wait. I would not have Mrs Maynard suffer the shock and the hurt of knowing the truth about Tony. She was an old lady and she was in very fragile health. She could not be expected to live more than a couple of years. Tony would keep.

On top of it all, it may not have been either Tony or Lesleigh who made those payments to Janet, let alone murdered her, and if I told the police what I knew, I might have done Heaven alone knew what damage for no useful purpose. I could do Janet Chisholm no good. In the end, I would have to do all I could to help expose her murderer, but for the moment it would all have to wait.

An owl hooted in soft repetition in the distance.

What would Tony do about this girl who was coming out from England? He couldn't afford to let her come. But how would he try to stop her? He *must* try to stop her. Probably he would take Mrs Maynard's letter in pretense of posting it, and quietly destroy it. Then Glenda Forbes' failure to answer Mrs Maynard's invitation would be put down to bad manners; and Glenda Forbes, for her part, would decide that Mrs Maynard either was too ill to answer her letter or the address was no longer correct, and almost certainly Glenda would not come. Tony might well substitute a letter himself – a letter purporting to be from Mrs Maynard – fobbing the girl off by giving her a false address for Tony, or telling her he had gone to New Zealand, or America, or anywhere far from Fairfield.

Tired and dispirited I went indoors and went to bed.

Seven

To my bewilderment Tony made no attempt to intercept Mrs Maynard's letter to Glenda Forbes. She gave it to me the next morning as I was going into Hobart to do some routine household shopping and Tony, who was present, took not the slightest notice. I expected him to offer to post the mail for me, but he didn't. Whatever plan he had formulated – and I was sure he must have a plan – it didn't include intercepting Glenda Forbes' mail.

Ashley Maclean phoned me that night.

"Anne, there's something I want to talk about. Would you let me drive you up the Derwent River valley? There's a delightful place where we can have lunch, and the scenery generally is very attractive. Could Mrs Maynard spare you on Saturday or Sunday, if you'd come?"

"Of course I'll come," I told him, "if Mrs Maynard feels well enough to do without me for the day."

Mrs Maynard assured me she was very happy for me to go out, so Ashley came about ten and we drove up through Hobart and on to New Norfolk up the Derwent valley on a day of sun and showers mixed brightly, when the river was brown in the rain and sparkling blue in the sun as it wound through country green with pastures and hop-fields and orchards.

We talked easily and comfortably and no mention was made of the night we had driven to the top of Mt Wellington until we visited the fish-hatchery so picturesquely set at Plenty. We strolled among the fish-ponds, down the paths bordered with the green torches of Lombardy poplars and in a quiet spot where there were no tourists gazing at the growing trout Ashley stopped and looked down at me, his eyes serious.

"I told you there was something I wanted to say. I'm afraid I owe you an apology for the way I behaved the other night when we went to dinner. To be honest, I hardly realized at the time that I'd done anything odd, but later – after I got home – I realized I'd driven very fast for quite a way, and rather behaved as if there was no-one else in the car."

He gave a faint smile. "That was unpardonable. I couldn't live with my thoughts at that moment, so I drove as if I were running second at Le Mans just so I'd have to concentrate on driving and forget everything else."

I touched his arm. "There's no need to apologize – or if there is, I think I'm the one who should be apologizing. I made you remember something you couldn't bear to remember. I'm sorry."

He was looking at me intently but his face was unreadable. "Someone told you? About my father and brother?"

I nodded. "Since then. I didn't know about it then, or before, when I asked you about the fire. I would never have made you talk about it."

He turned partly away and stood looking down at the pond where young trout swam idly.

"It doesn't usually get to me like that now. Most times I can talk about the fire objectively. But sometimes it just jumps at me when I'm off guard. You know I sent them to die?"

"You couldn't know what would happen. A fire like that is completely unpredictable. You could only do what seemed to be right – what *was* right in the circumstances. The circumstances changed, that's all."

He squatted down on his haunches, his slender figure looking deceptively fragile and unlike a hard-working orchardist. I wanted desperately to reach him with some sort of comforting words, but I felt even my clumsy attempt had fallen on deaf ears. To the group of tourists who came chattering by, he must have appeared just another visitor absorbedly interested in the fish.

Presently, when the little knot of people went on by, Ashley stood up and looked at me.

"Thank you, Anne. I guess what you say is true. But my father and Donald trusted my judgment and my judgment was wrong. At the time all I could think of was the fact that my mother was alone right in the path of the fire. I knew the main road was cut by the fire, but the lane was clear. It just never occurred to me that the fire could change direction and cut the lane so quickly."

"If your own car had started, you'd have been trapped, too."

"Yes." He stubbed at the concrete pool-surround with the toe of his shoe. "Did whoever told you the story hint that maybe I made sure my car wouldn't start, in order to guarantee that I wouldn't be caught if things got nasty?"

"No!" I said sharply. "Why should anyone think that?"

He shrugged. "People must sometimes wonder if I took the safe way."

"No one would think that! No one who knows you."

He smiled and for a few moments just stood looking at me. "What a nice person you are."

He turned away. "I'd always wanted Oakhill, or a share in it, but it wasn't big enough for both Donald and me as well as our parents. Donald was older by four years and it was always taken for granted that he'd be the one to take up a partnership with Dad, and ultimately own Oakhill. Donald was just as keen on the place as I was, but he was –"

His voice shook for a second. "He was a jolly decent fellow and he knew we both wanted Oakhill, and he wasn't such a traditionalist as our parents, so he suggested what might seem a very peculiar solution. He suggested we toss for it."

He smiled again, a little wryly. "It might seem odd to stake your whole future career on the flip of a coin, but it seemed to both of us the only completely fair way. I lost, and chose to become a high-school teacher, which appealed as the next-best thing. I was just about ready to start my second year at university when the fire came. For a while then I came very close to hating Oakhill. If my mother hadn't been anxious for me to stay on and keep the place I think I'd never have set foot on it again."

There was a little silence and then I said, "You love it now."

"Oh, yes. I love it now. And don't think you can't ask questions, Anne, or talk about the fire. It would be no use to try to act as if it had never happened. It can never be shut out of my mind and it's much better to talk about it naturally and openly. I don't usually carry on like a maniac the way I did the other night. I must have given you the very devil of a fright. I'm sorry."

I took his arm and we walked back to the car in silence, but it was an unconstrained silence.

We had an excellent lunch and looked at a couple of old buildings and wandered through the appealing countryside, stopping now and then to get out of the car and walk beside the river during breaks between the wind-scudded showers, or look at the hop-fields, in relaxed and companionable easiness.

When Ashley drove me home he came in to see Mrs Maynard. "I'd like you and Anne to come over to Oakhill for lunch one day soon," he told her. "My cleaning lady is willing to prepare lunch for visitors whenever I want her to. You haven't been to Oakhill for ages, and Anne has never seen it. I'd like your opinion of the way I've kept the garden."

"That would be pleasant," Mrs Maynard said warmly, and went on to tell Ashley about Glenda Forbes' proposed visit.

I wonder, I thought: Tony must have some plan for stopping her, but since he hadn't taken the obvious step of preventing Mrs Maynard's letter from being posted I had no idea what his plan might be.

It was arranged that Mrs Maynard and I would go to lunch on the following Tuesday week, and it was on the morning of that visit that Glenda Forbes' letter came. Mrs Maynard read it aloud to Tony and me.

Glenda declared herself absolutely delighted to receive the invitation to stay and thanked Mrs Maynard with pleasant enthusiasm. She had checked airline schedules through a travel agent and would come on to Hobart as soon as she could get on a connecting flight from Sydney.

She followed that remark with dates and times. She would arrive in Sydney on the morning of the Saturday after our scheduled visit to Oakhill, and would arrive in Hobart later in the day.

I looked at Tony. "I'll drive in to Hobart airport and pick her up, if you like," I said. "You're pretty busy on the orchard, with spraying and thinning."

"Sure," he said readily. "Thanks."

If he had said: "There's an unexploded hand-grenade just behind you," I could scarcely have been more flabbergasted.

I had been so certain that as he hadn't tried to stop Mrs Maynard's letter of invitation from being sent, certainly he must have intended to be the first to meet Glenda – to do just what, I had no idea. Now it seemed he wasn't even anxious to do that. Yet how could he dare to let her come, since she must inevitably expose his masquerade?

I couldn't stop turning the problem over and over in my mind over the next few days. It preoccupied me even on our visit to Oakhill, though it did retreat into the recesses of my brain while I explored the gardens.

The relationship between Oakhill and Fairfield was readily discernible even on first sight. The house was not as large as Fairfield but was built of the same stone, with flagstoned verandahs on two sides and leaded diamond-paned windows. As Drew Thomas had told me, the same idea of isolating the farm sheds and seasonal-workers' cottages from sight of the house was repeated with the long-ago planting of elms and oaks and a hawthorn hedge. It was true, too, that Oakhill didn't have Fairfield's splendid views, though it had a pleasant outlook over its own orchard and down a little valley where the sun glinted on water, to another farm beyond.

But while Fairfield's garden was pleasant, Oakhill's was superb.

As I stepped from the car and Ashley came out to greet us I exclaimed involuntarily, "What wonderful gardens!"

Almost a hectare of gently-sloping land was planted with native trees mixed with Japanese maples, liquidambers, rhododendrons, azaleas, roses, native heath and a whole conglomerate of edging plants and low-growing shrubs filling areas under the trees and making a foreground for them. The whole was most cleverly designed, with lawns and paths used to make the most of the natural fall of the land.

"You've kept it up splendidly, Ashley," Mrs Maynard told him as he helped her out of the car.

He smiled. "Fay chose the things she planted with great care, in order to minimize the work once the garden was established. My wife," he explained to me. "The garden was always quite large, and of course all the big trees you see were planted long ago, probably by the original owners. But Fay saw the possibilities of turning it into something rather lovely, and she promptly set about putting her ideas into practice."

"She must have had the eye of a true artist," I said, and

meant it.

"Why don't you show Anne around the garden, Ashley?" Mrs Maynard suggested. "I shall sit in one of the chairs on the verandah and admire it from a little distance in comfort, and I assure you that if I see anything to criticize I shall bring it to your attention." She smiled, and we went out across the lawn.

"Was your wife a professional landscape designer?" I asked.

He shook his head. "She was a laboratory technician. But she loved beauty and could often see it where most people wouldn't – or could see where the most mundane things could be made beautiful."

I slid my hand under the tip of a branch of Japanese maple and let the delicate multi-pointed leaves lie for a moment against my palm. "Did she live to see the maturing of the work she had done here?"

"Enough to derive a good deal of pleasure from it, and satisfaction. And almost to the end she managed to go on doing a little work in it."

We walked in silence for a minute or two, and then he said, "It's interesting that this friend of Tony's should be coming out."

I shot a glance at him, wondering if something beyond idle comment lay behind the remark. "Yes," I said noncommittally.

"I gather from what Mrs Maynard said," Ashley went on, "that they can't have been such very close friends, because apparently they haven't been in touch for years. Just seems a little strange that she should suddenly decide to look him up."

"Oh, I don't know. She's been in Canada and they just lost touch. I think often it's only when you're about to arrive in a strange place that you realize it's rather nice to think there's someone there who isn't a total stranger."

"You had no-one, did you?" It was more a statement than a question. "Were you very lonely?"

"At times," I said. For the second time I was strongly tempted to tell him the truth; and for the second time I was sufficiently cautious to hold my tongue.

It was one of those absurd small accidents which should never happen.

It was the day before Glenda Forbes was due to arrive, and I was sweeping the porch at the back door, my back turned to the single step. I was still waiting for Tony to make a move to meet Glenda first, and alone, though what he expected to be able to do anyway I had no idea – except that I was certain he had a plan, and one in which he had great confidence.

Drew Thomas had driven his elderly but cherished little car out after school and had been in to talk with Mrs Maynard. As he came out through the kitchen he called to me, "Can I have a couple of these smashing-looking cookie things, Anne, or are they all members of a protected species, being jealously guarded as a welcome-to-the-colonies treat for Tony's old flame?"

"I don't know about being a protected species but they'll certainly be an endangered species if you get loose among them. All right, you may have two."

"Would you believe three?" he said blithely, coming out on to the porch munching.

"Glutton," I told him.

"Rubbish. I'm just paying your culinary arts a compliment. I'm dying to meet Tony's bit of skirt, aren't you? Has he let drop any hint what she looks like? Vital statistics? Age?"

"No. And I'd be a bit doubtful about the 'bit of skirt' description. Don't forget they haven't even written in over two years."

I looked at Drew, taking in the alert, intelligent face, the humorous mouth and the indefinable thing about his eyes which I would have described as kindness. Not for the first time, I wanted to tell him the whole story. This quick-witted boy could be a valuable ally; but I had no right to ease my burden by loading some of it on to his shoulders.

I resumed my sweeping. "Anyway, he was quite happy to jump at my offer to go and meet her at the airport tomorrow, so if she was his bit of skirt once it must have been –"

I stepped backwards off the edge of the porch, caught the side of my foot on the step and went sprawling in a singularly undignified tangle of legs and arms.

Drew jumped forward and knelt concernedly beside me. "Anne! Are you hurt?"

I sat up. "I think I've wrenched my ankle a bit, but I haven't done any other damage, I'm sure. It was only such a little way to fall I really shouldn't have hurt anything but my pride. I must have been born clumsy to have fallen at all."

I gave him my hand and he helped me to my feet, but I found on cautious experimentation that I could scarcely bear to put any weight on my right foot.

"Are you sure you haven't broken anything?" Drew demanded.

I shook my head. "No, it's not that bad – just a sprain. I'll bathe it in some cold water and bandage it up and it'll be all right, but I suspect I'll be a bit hobbledy for a couple of days."

The ankle, duly bathed and bandaged, was indeed quite painful to walk on, but I could still get around with difficulty. It did raise one problem: it was most unlikely I would be able to drive a car with any degree of safety for a few days, which meant I couldn't meet Glenda Forbes' flight at the airport next afternoon. I was distressed at the thought and furious with myself for falling victim to such a stupid mishap, but I kept hoping that by next day it would have improved enough to let me drive.

Somehow, I must contrive to see Glenda first, to warn her, urge her to co-operate with me; at least to make sure Mrs Maynard wasn't present when Glenda and Tony first met and Glenda blurted out that he was not Tony at all. I wondered what in the world the girl would think, or say, when Tony met her at the airport if I wasn't able to drive. And I couldn't imagine what Tony would say to *her*, even though I had spent a good many sleepless hours trying to imagine it.

By lunchtime on Saturday I had to admit to myself that though a bandage and a spare walking-stick belonging to Mrs Maynard just enabled me to limp around, my ankle, swollen and painful, made it temporarily impossible for me to drive the car.

I said so, apologetically, during lunch. Tony shrugged. "Well, never mind. I'd better do the gentlemanly thing and meet her myself."

"I'll go if you like," Drew volunteered. "If you're busy."

Tony looked at him for a moment. "All right," he agreed. "If you don't mind. It would save me losing the afternoon and I'd like to get this lot of spraying done in case the weather breaks."

Drew grinned. "For an old flame, you're awfully casual."

"Old flame?" Tony laughed. "A flame long put out, then. You're as bad as Grandma, dreaming that it's the revival of a long-lost romance."

I was still baffled. Again Tony had been presented with the perfect reason for going to meet Glenda, and again he had casually let it pass. I looked at his unconcerned face and wondered desperately what was going on in his mind.

It was about five o'clock in the brightly sunlit summer evening when the sound of the car in the drive ended my listening vigil. Tony had been in for a cup of tea a little before four and had gone out again and not returned. Mrs Maynard was waiting in the lounge, having postponed her afternoon tea so that she and Glenda could have it together.

"You must join us, Anne. You and Glenda are probably much of an age. She'll be tired after such a long flight and no doubt will want to get to bed as soon after dinner as possible, but a cup of tea is a very satisfactory welcome in a new place and among strangers."

Stick in hand, I limped to the front door as a young woman, perhaps a year or two older than I was, got out of the car and ran a quick, appraising look over the house. She was of medium height, inclined to slight plumpness, and had a fair-skinned, dark-haired prettiness. In spite of her long flight Glenda looked alert and interested and I heard her exclaim to Drew:

"It's perfectly charming!" Then she saw me and came forward. "You're Anne, of course. Drew has been telling me about your mishap. I'm sorry about your ankle. I'll be able to help around the house and make things a little easier for you, I hope."

"Thank you. I'll be fully active again in a few days, I'm sure. You must be fearfully tired and want nothing more than to rest and catch up on some sleep, so we've planned an early dinner. Come and meet Mrs Maynard and have a cup of tea. She's looking forward to meeting you."

I ushered her into the lounge where Mrs Maynard rose in welcome. With Drew standing on the verandah, suitcases in hand, and Mrs Maynard waiting to greet her guest, it was no time to try to launch into an explanation that the man who would presently come in was not the friend she had come to meet – even if I'd known how to tell her.

Glenda was very pleasant to Mrs Maynard and remarked with enthusiasm on the charm of Fairfield and chatted about the flight out and how outrageous her English winter clothes had seemed when she got to Sydney, and all the time I tried to contribute whatever seemed necessary to the conversation while listening for the sound of the tractor heralding Tony's return. There was nothing left for me to do now but try to ensure Mrs Maynard was not present when Glenda and Tony met. What might happen after that I couldn't anticipate. I simply felt a kind of dull, fatalistic acceptance that there was nothing more that I could do for the moment.

To my profound relief Mrs Maynard suggested that as Glenda would no doubt like to shower and change, she herself would go to her room for a rest before dinner; to save my ankle, Drew would show Glenda her room.

I was in the kitchen getting dinner under way when I heard the sound of the tractor as Tony came in from the orchard, just as I heard a step in the hallway and Glenda came in, looking refreshed from a shower and wearing a summer dress.

"Oh, I do feel better," she said feelingly. "Will that be Tony coming in?"

"Yes," I said. I was swamped with a bleak sense of helplessness and anger at my own inadequacy. Now there was nothing left for me to do but stand back and wait to see how Tony was going to cope with the situation.

"Oh, good. I'll go out and meet him," Glenda said.

She went quickly out through the back door and across the lawn as the tractor came up the drive, Tony dressed in khaki overalls with a wide-brimmed hat shading his face against the late sun. I stood as if mesmerized at the sink, watching. Glenda waved to him and he waved back, stopped the tractor and jumped off, sweeping off his hat so that the sun spilled over his fair hair and handsome tanned face.

Glenda ran to him without a moment's hesitation, took his outstretched hands and reached up to kiss him on the cheek.

"Tony!" I heard her say, laughing. "What ages it's been!"

He stood grinning down at her. "Canada agreed with you," he said. "You're blooming."

They stood chatting and laughing easily while I gripped the edge of the kitchen sink for support that had nothing to do with my injured ankle. The world had gone into a moment of dizzy revolving.

I knew now why Tony had been so unconcerned at the prospect of Glenda's arrival. He wanted it. He had undoubtedly planned it.

Because there was no question about it: they knew each other. Glenda Forbes had not come here expecting to meet Tony Maynard. She had come knowing she was to meet an imposter. The charming little scene of the reunion of old friends was as deliberately staged for effect as a West End first night.

Glenda Forbes was cover – a confirmation of Tony Maynard – and her arrival was designed to give depth and strength to his identity. It meant one of two things: either he was keen on the girl and wanted her with him and thought he was firmly enough established to bring her on to the scene; or he was going to extraordinary lengths to strengthen his position and confirm himself as unquestionably the man he claimed to be.

It was good cover: the reunion with an old friend made the identification convincing to the last degree from the human viewpoint. It was clever. Whether it was necessary was debatable, but it was certainly an indication of how seriously Tony took his impersonation and how much planning and thought he had put into it.

But still it didn't fully cover him if his plan was to inherit Fairfield – and obviously it was. Surely he would still have to produce certain documents for the relevant authorities as routine confirmation of identity.

Somehow I made myself go on with the preparations to serve dinner as soon as Tony had showered and changed. Somehow I had to act naturally in my role as housekeeper which in the circumstances placed me in the position of largely undertaking to be hostess.

And I had to do it in the knowledge that now I no longer was dealing with an imposter. Now I had to deal with two in conspiracy.

Eight

Glenda was bright, chatty and entirely pleasant both to Mrs Maynard and to me. It was obvious that she was exactly what she said she was: by occupation a shorthand-typist who had worked for some time in Canada – long enough to pick up a faint Canadian accent. She was ready and happy to help around the house and she genuinely did relieve me of a good deal of the work and allowed me to rest my injured ankle, and for that I was grateful.

I spent more time with Mrs Maynard and I felt that in that time I got to know her better than in the previous months I'd been at Fairfield. Christmas was almost on us, and I helped her with her mail and her personal shopping, and we also planned household shopping because it was her habit to invite Drew and his parents, Ashley Maclean and his mother – who, it seemed, was still strong enough to leave the nursing home for a few hours occasionally – to share a mid-day Christmas dinner. As well, it was traditional to invite most of the neighbours in groups of a dozen or so for after-dinner drinks and savouries and a chat on evenings scattered over the week or two before Christmas.

We had been discussing these arrangement one day when Mrs Maynard said unexpectedly: "Tell me, Anne, what do you think of Glenda?"

I smiled faintly. "Are you asking me if I think she would be a suitable wife for Tony? I don't really think there's any romance."

"Perhaps not."

"Do *you* think she'd be a suitable wife?" I countered.

"I don't know. She's very pleasant, but I'm not sure she'd be really right for Tony. She – I don't think she's *strong* enough. I think – I think she'd be too ready to do whatever Tony wanted. Tony might think that's grand, and that worries me a little. Because I don't think a strong character and a weak one are likely to be happy for long. The strong character can get very tired of weakness, in time, and the weak get tired of being trampled. Do you think she's in love with him?"

"Hardly. After all, she hasn't bothered to try to keep in touch with him for over two years. But she might have been, once. Or he with her."

The closer relationship which grew up between my grandmother and me over those few days of my partial incapacitation was a thing I greatly valued, but it was obvious, as it always had been, that she had an autocratic side to her nature which probably helped her to defy her physical weakness. Whether she had developed it in defiance of that weakness or whether it had always been a part of her nature I wasn't sure.

Schools closed for the long Christmas vacation, and Drew spent at least half of his time at Fairfield. Once I was properly on my feet again Glenda left for a week-long coach tour of southern Tasmania with all the enthusiasm of a keen tourist. "I'd like to see some more of this state before the apple season begins," she told me. "Tony has suggested that since I'm looking for work I might like to try out here on Fairfield as a seasonal worker before I look for something permanent, and I must say I think it would be rather fun."

I drove her into Hobart to board the coach, and when I arrived back at Fairfield Ashley's station-sedan was parked in the driveway and he was in the lounge talking to Mrs Maynard. He came out through the kitchen as he was leaving.

I said, "I hope your mother's well enough to come on Christmas Day."

He smiled. "I hope so, too. I'd like you to meet her. She's very frail, but clear in her mind and I'm sure she'd like you a great deal."

We chatted for a moment and he asked me where Tony was.

"I'm not sure. There was a fellow arrived just as I left to take Glenda into Hobart – had new tyres to fit on the tractor – and Tony and Drew went down to the machinery shed with him. I heard Tony ask Drew if he'd take the tractor when it was ready and do some slashing on the southern hill, but I don't know where Tony was going. He may still be around the sheds."

Ashely nodded. "I'll go across and look."

It was perhaps fifteen minutes later that I decided I would go over to the huts which served as accommodation for the seasonal workers and open them up and see how much attention they needed in the way of cleaning, to be ready for the start of the apple-picking season. The first Gravensteins, Tony had said, would be ready to pick in about five or six weeks.

As I passed the machinery shed, Ashley stepped out. "Find Tony?" I called.

He looked at me sharply as if surprised to see me. "No. I've looked in the shed, but he and Drew seem to have disappeared."

"Is the tractor still there?"

"Yes, but the Landrover's gone, so they must have gone off in that. Never mind – it wasn't important."

He went back to his car and I went on to the cabins, which were austere but reasonably comfortable. Everything was covered with a fine film of dust and I set about opening the windows to air the cabins while I went back to the house for brooms and buckets and scrubbing brushes to begin the cleaning chores. There was a communal shower-and-toilet block which also would have to be checked.

I was still working on the first hut when I heard the Landrover return and presently Tony and Drew came to the door of the cabin. "Bit early cleaning up, aren't you?" Tony said. "The dust will all settle over things again before the seasonals move in."

"Some will," I agreed, "but it'll be easy enough to cope with. Ashley was here looking for you. I thought you might still have been around the machinery shed, but he said you weren't. He said it wasn't important."

They went off and I returned to my cleaning. Presently I heard the tractor start up and go, but it was such a routine sound I barely even registered it. By the time I'd finished cleaning the first hut it was time to prepare lunch and I went across to the house and busied myself about the kitchen.

Tony came in and I gave him his lunch of cold meat and salad, and took Mrs Maynard's to her room as she said she was feeling tired and the day was quite hot. Drew wasn't home and I said I'd wait my lunch for him.

He still wasn't home when Tony was ready to go back to work and he said, "Drew's late. Hope he hasn't had trouble with the tractor. It's not like him to run late for meals. I just hope he didn't break a slasher blade on a rock and put the broken bit through one those new back tyres."

As he spoke, Drew walked around the drive from the sheds. I began to turn away to get his lunch and mine on to the table, and then I wheeled back.

"Drew! What's happened? Are you hurt?"

His shirt was torn and he was muddied and limping and there was an ugly bruise on his cheek. He shook his head. "I'm all right. I don't think the tractor's much damaged, but she did roll."

"What the devil happened?" Tony demanded. "I know the slope's a fair grade, but how the hell did you roll it?"

Drew pulled off his cap and flopped into a kitchen chair. "Elementary, my dear Watson," he said, but there was no flippancy in his face. "A wheel came off."

"A – what?" Tony snapped. "How in hell could it?" He was staring at Drew, tense and angry. "Wheels don't just come off tractors."

Drew looked pale and shocked. "This one did. Sorry, Tony."

"It's not your fault," I said quietly. "Tony, get me some first-aid gear. Drew's got some cuts on his hands and that's a nasty knock on the cheek. Never mind the tractor for the moment. Drew, are you sure you're all right? Shall I get you to a doctor?"

"No, of course not," he said impatiently. "I just feel such a blasted idiot, that's all."

Tony was getting bandages and sticking-plaster out of a high cupboard in the kitchen while I took ice-cubes from the refrigerator and put them in a bowl, sat Drew in a chair and examined the cuts and abrasions to his arm and shoulder. None of the cuts proved to be serious, but he would be stiff and sore for a few days. I bathed the bruise on his face with iced water and asked:

"Were you knocked out?"

He shook his head. "The thing just threw me clear as it turned over, and I did a couple more fast rolls for good measure, but it was good luck rather than good management on my part that got me clear. The only thing I could think of was to scramble up and turn the ignition off."

"Good thing you kept your head enough to do that," Tony said. "Is the tractor upside down?"

"Afraid so. But there really doesn't seem to be much damage. I think somebody with another tractor could pull it back on its wheels without much bother."

"I'll phone Ashley and ask him if he can come over," Tony said. "Though what I should do is call a tow-truck out from town and present the bill to that addle-headed bloody idiot from the tyre company."

"Why?" I asked.

"Why? Because the brainless fool didn't tighten the wheel nuts after he put the new tyres on, of course!" Tony snapped. "He couldn't have."

"Good Lord!" I said. "I'd forgotten for the moment that someone had put new tyres on. But that's dreadful carelessness! Drew might have been killed."

"So," Tony said, "I intend to point out to them rather forcibly at the earliest suitable moment. But the first thing is to check up on the tractor. I'll call Ashley."

"Hang on a bit and I'll go back to the tractor with you," Drew said.

"No," I said firmly. "You're going to eat. I'm still not entirely sure you shouldn't see a doctor."

"Oh, hogwash," Drew said impatiently. "I'm perfectly all right and, after all, I was the one who rolled it. I should go back and pick up the pieces."

"No one could have stopped it from rolling if it suddenly lost a wheel on that slope," I told him. "And you've had a very nasty shock. You're going to have a meal and a rest."

"Anne's right," Tony said somewhat unexpectedly. "It wasn't any way your fault." He went out to phone Ashley, and presently came back through the kitchen to say that Ashley would go straight to the scene of the accident with his tractor; Tony was going now in the Landrover.

As we ate our lunch, Drew was oddly quiet. I would have expected him to want to talk about the accident, but he was unusually silent and seemed preoccupied. He helped me with the washing-up and when I went back to clean out another fruitpickers' cabin he followed me as if he had something on his mind.

I waited, not wanting to try to force him into a confidence, wondering uneasily whether in fact the tractor accident somehow *had* been his fault, and he had been unwilling to admit it to Tony. Yet it wasn't like Drew to dodge responsibility.

Presently, after he had wandered around the hut three times absentmindedly, I pulled out a chair and sat down. "All right," I said, "suppose you tell me what's weighing so heavily on your painful conscience."

He swung around to look at me. "I guess it was obvious,

wasn't it?"

"Horribly," I agreed.

He leaned back against the wall and fingered his bruised cheek gingerly.

"Anne," he said slowly, "you said Ashley came here this morning, looking for Tony."

"Yes."

"What did he do?"

"Do ? Well, when I came back from taking Glenda in to catch the bus, he was in talking to Mrs Maynard. Then he went out to see if Tony was around, and when I came over to start cleaning the first cabin he said the Landrover was gone and there was no sign of Tony, so he went. Why?"

"How long was he here?"

"I don't know." I frowned, puzzled. "I suppose he'd been here a while when I came home."

Drew shook his head. "No, I mean how long was he down *here*, around the sheds?"

"A while," I said. "I remember being a bit surprised that he'd spent so much time looking for Tony – fifteen minutes or so, I suppose. But why?"

"So he could have been in the machinery shed."

"Oh, he was," I agreed. "He was just coming out when I came down here."

Drew said nothing, and I looked at him hard. "Drew, why do you want to know?"

He stood very still for a silent minute. I waited. Outside, I remember, a blackbird sang with a tumbling gaiety of sound.

"I shouldn't tell you, Anne," Drew said unhappily. "But I've got to tell someone."

"That's all right," I said with a brightness that was a denial of the sudden coldness I felt stealing through me. "First cousin to a clam, that's me. Now, sit down and tell Aunty all about it."

He neither sat down nor made any attempt at his usual banter. "I've got to ask you to hold your tongue, Anne, because I – I don't know what to do. I never have, so I've kept quiet."

"I'll hold my tongue," I told him quietly. After a pause I added, "It's Ashley, isn't it? I've held my tongue over what you told me, partly because it's not for me to tell anyone, anyway; partly because I don't know what it meant. One can jump to conclusions which might be very wrong conclusions."

He nodded. "But there was more to it than I told you. You see, Janet Chisholm was blackmailing Ashley. Or at least, she was trying to."

The meaning of what he had said took several seconds to register, and I stared at him in horrified astonishment. "*Blackmailing*? Ashley? Why?"

"She asked him what he would do if she told him she could prove he was a murderer."

"*What*?" I gasped.

"That," Drew said grimly, "is exactly what Ashley said."

There was a little silence. I took a long breath.

"Drew," I said slowly, "I think you'd better begin at the beginning. How do you know this?"

"I lied when I said I'd just gone for a walk the morning after Janet was killed. You see, I knew she wasn't home. I'd been outside to let Buzz off the chain, and I saw her car wasn't there. So I went to her room and saw she wasn't there, either."

He ran a hand through his hair. "It wasn't any coincidence that I saw Ashley with those clothes of his with blood on them. I went straight to his place. I don't know what I expected to find. Janet's car, maybe. Some evidence she'd been there. I don't know. I was scared sick. I was scared sick that she was dead."

I was staring at him still in bewilderment. "But why? Why, because Janet was missing, did you think Ashley might have killed her? Why did you think she was blackmailing him?"

"Because I heard her, just a few weeks before. I'd gone for a walk. It was a Sunday afternoon and I hadn't seen Ashley for a while so I thought I'd stop by his place and say hello – he'd probably be working in the garden. When I got near the house I saw a wheelbarrow down near a rhododendron hedge and I guessed he must be down there, so I went down.

"It wasn't till I got close that I realized he had someone with him, and when I recognized Janet's voice I didn't want to interrupt, so I was just about to turn around and go away again when I heard her say it, just like that. They'd been talking in an ordinary sort of way as I walked down – I couldn't hear what they were saying, nor I didn't even recognize the voices till I was just on the other side of the hedge. I could hear the snip of secateurs as Ashley was evidently doing some pruning, and there was a little lull in the conversation. They hadn't heard my footsteps, apparently – or certainly Janet hadn't – because I hadn't walked down the path, just taken a shortcut across the lawn."

He paused, not looking at me, his face troubled as if he were listening to the voices all over again.

"Janet spoke almost as casually as if she'd been commenting on the weather: 'I've something to ask you, Ashley.' 'Ask away,' Ashley said in a comfortable sort of way. I'll swear he had no more idea than I did what she was going to say. 'What would you do,' Janet said, 'if I told you I am witness to the fact that you're a murderer?'

"I think I froze in mid-step," Drew went on. "They couldn't see me, of course, because I was on the other side of the rhododendrons. Ashley said, as if he was sure he hadn't heard correctly: '*What*?' She didn't answer at once, and he said in a queer kind of voice, 'What did you say?' 'Oh, I'm perfectly serious,' Janet said. 'I can stand up in court and swear that you're a murderer.'

"Everything went quiet. I hardly dared to breathe. Then Ashley said in the same half-strangled sort of voice, 'And just who am I supposed to have murdered?' 'I don't think you need to be told,' Janet said. 'You've hardly forgotten how your father and brother died.' 'No,' Ashley said. 'I've hardly forgotten.' 'How do you sleep at nights?' Janet asked. 'Sometimes,' Ashley said, 'not very well.' "

Drew turned and looked at me.

"Do you know the story of how Ashley's father and brother were trapped in the bushfire?"

"Yes," I said. I felt frozenly numb. "Yes, I know."

Ashley, I thought. Oh, God. And even then I wasn't sure what I was really thinking, only that there was pain somewhere deep in me.

Drew said, "Ashley told her he had never denied being responsible for their deaths. 'I sent them to die,' he said, and he sounded as if he was hurting all over. 'I know that, and so does everyone. It's no secret. I did what I thought was right. You can call it stupidity, or you can call it ignorance, or you can just say it was one of those terrible freakish movements the fire made. But no one could call it murder.' 'Ah,' Janet said, 'but suppose I say it wasn't a mistake, wasn't ignorance?' Ashley asked her what in hell she was talking about.

"Janet said, 'I was there that day. I was on a visit with my mother to the people who owned that orchard at the time – the orchard you and your father and brother and the others were fighting for. We were staying for a week. But I was just a child and couldn't be expected to understand the significance of what I saw – not then; although it puzzled me a bit and it stuck in my mind, you see, and when I came back here to work it all came back to me.' 'And what did you see?' Ashley demanded. 'I saw you go out and look at the fire situation very carefully. And the lane you then went and told your father and brother to use *was already cut* by fire, though they couldn't see that from where they were working. The fire had *already* changed direction and anyone could see the whole lane would be on fire in minutes. You sent them into a trap, knowing it was a trap. You knew they couldn't get through. You had to make it look good, so you went to your car as if to follow them. But very conveniently it wouldn't start in time for you to go with them, and by the time you did get it going the lane was on fire from end to end'."

"No," I whispered, staring at Drew. "No."

He went on: "Ashley called her a filthy liar, and she laughed. 'Oh,' she said, 'cheer up, darling. It probably isn't evidence that could even get you arrested, let alone convicted, on a murder charge, because if it came to court the lawyers could probably dismiss the evidence as a child's misinterpretation, a memory dulled by time and therefore unreliable, and in any case it's only one person's word against another's. But arrests and convictions aside, it seems to me that everyone in the district knows that you wanted this orchard and always had wanted it. All I have to do is produce my story. There's nothing you can do against a rumour. You'd be finished. You couldn't go on living here with a rumour like that circulating. And besides, imagine what it would do to your mother.'

"Ashley's voice was as quiet as anything, but there was absolute fury in it. 'You wouldn't dare,' he said. Janet laughed. 'Oh, wouldn't I?' 'You're nothing but a bloody little liar,' Ashley told her. 'Really?' she said. 'Well, if you're so confident it's a lie, what are you worrying about? Besides, I'll hold my tongue over the whole affair, for a price. I'm a very considerate person. I want to be quite well paid, naturally, but I'll keep it within the bounds of what you can pay.'

"I was standing there feeling as if someone had hit me in the stomach with a sledge-hammer," Drew said. "I gathered up my wits enough to know I'd better get out of there before they saw me, so I cleared off without waiting to hear any more. I just felt I wanted to go away and be sick."

He sat down in the chair across the table from me and looked at me. "So you see why I got such a devil of a jolt when I saw Ashley with blood on his clothes."

"Drew," I said shakenly, "why haven't you told the police?"

"Because it could be nearly enough to get Ashley convicted on a murder charge, almost entirely on my say-so. And it's not on, Anne. I won't do it. Because it can still be all wrong. He probably just told Janet to get lost – called her bluff – and she backed off. It probably had nothing to do with her death."

I said hoarsely, "Someone was paying her blackmail." I told him about the deposits in Janet's bank account.

"Hell!" Drew said. He added after a minute, "But it mightn't have been Ashley who was paying. If she tried to blackmail him she might have tried it with goodness knows how many others. Because nothing she said to Ashley need have been true. I don't think it was. I got the impression that she was only taunting him. And even if he felt he had to pay her to keep her filthy mouth closed, it doesn't prove he was guilty of murder – *any* murder."

I said, "If he wasn't guilty of killing his father and brother, why would he agree to pay blackmail?"

"Because what Janet said was right. *Legally* he was safe enough. But once she circulated the rumour, whether any of it was true or not, how could Ashley go on living here with his neighbours wondering every time they looked at him whether he really was a murderer? And there was his mother, an invalid who'd had enough traumas. Oh, it was a good thing Janet was on to, and I guess she knew it. Ashley would have been forced to keep her quiet. One way or another."

We sat for several minutes, not looking at each other.

Then I said bleakly, "You think Ashley might have tampered with that tractor wheel, don't you? Why?"

"Because I can't see an experienced tyre-man failing to tighten home those wheel-nuts. Suppose Ashley *did* see me, either the day Janet was threatening him or the morning I saw him with blood-stained clothes? He wouldn't know how much I knew, and he might decide I was dangerous to have around. If he did kill Janet. He'd know I was likely to be the first one to use the tractor because I like to get on to any tractor work that's going when I'm here. He probably would know that I'd been doing some slashing down on that slope and would probably be going back to it. And it might have worked Anne," he said in a tight voice. "I was just plain lucky, unless there's special Providence looks after fools. I was thrown clear as the tractor rolled, but it could have rolled on me, and it damned near did."

He leapt up. "Oh, damn and damn!" he said bitterly, and strode out of the hut and away, limping a little, without another glance at me.

I went on sitting there, staring at nothing, my mind a whirl of bewilderment.

There seemed little doubt that Janet Chisholm had been a singularly unpleasant person who had not hesitated to supplement her income by blackmail. I had believed that here she had had two possible targets: Tony, if she had somehow discovered he was an imposter; and, more probably to my way of thinking, Lesleigh Martin with her drug addiction. Both might well be dangerous if cornered.

Now I had been faced with a third prospect. Ashley. I could never believe he had deliberately sent his father and brother to die, perhaps because I couldn't accept that anyone so monstrous could even look like a normal human being, let alone behave like one. And there I let myself commit a basic error.

Yet even if he was totally innocent of his father's and brother's deaths, Janet's threat to unleash an unproven but totally indefensible accusation against him might be enough to rouse almost any man to blindly murderous fury.

Like Drew, I wanted to believe it was not Ashley. But –

I sat bolt upright with a start.

Drew!

Never once had I considered him as a suspect in Janet's murder, and yet of course he must be. He was at Fairfield the night Janet was killed, and so had to be considered along with everyone else.

He was the person who had told me two damning stories about Ashley – stories where *he was the only witness*.

I sat still, horrified at the trend of my own thoughts. Drew was no more than a boy. In the few months I had known him I had become very fond of him. The mere thought of him being a murderer – let alone trying to set up a story to frame someone else – was sickening. And what possible motive could he have had for killing Janet? She couldn't have been blackmailing him, because not only could I not imagine what fearful secret Drew could have, it was absurd to think a final-year high school student with barely enough money to put petrol in his decrepit car could pay out five hundred dollars a week to a blackmailer.

No. Blackmail was out as a motive, so what was left? An unrequited boyish passion for an older woman? Ridiculous. But was it? How could I know? And was it possible that his story of Janet's attempt to blackmail Ashley was true, and out of the very real friendship he apparently felt for Ashley he had been motivated by anger to destroy Janet's grasping evil?

But then why try to make me believe Ashley was the killer, if the murder itself had been done to *protect* Ashley?

I put my head in my hands as if I could shut out the whole monstrous thing from my thoughts. It was still possible, I told myself, that Janet's blackmail money – if that's what it was – had come from some other source altogether. Someone out of her past life could have been the person who was paying her, and that same person may have arranged to meet her that night, ostensibly to make another payment, and when Janet had kept the ugly rendezvous her victim had become her killer. For the blood on Ashley's clothes there was some other other explanation.

I got up and began to go on with the cleaning of the fruit-pickers' cabin. Somehow, to stop myself from weeping, I would work, and cling to my hope; a stranger was the murderer.

Nine

At breakfast the day after the tractor accident Tony asked me if I'd like to go to the casino that night.

The invitation was so unexpected that I thought perhaps I'd misheard him, and I stared at him with an astonishment which bordered on rudeness.

"Well?" he said quizzically with a sardonic lift of an eyebrow. "We can have a flutter at the tables, watch other people's changing fortunes when we've made ours, then have supper and come home. What's in all that to make you look as if I were an Arab sheik who'd just asked you to become his one-hundred-and-twenty-third wife?"

"Sorry," I said hastily. "Yes, thank you, I'd like to go. It was just that you took me by surprise, that's all. I mean, you've never asked me out before, and then – well, there's Glenda –"

He laughed in real amusement. "I'm asking *you* out, not Glenda. You can just put it down to the spirit of Christmas approaching, or you can attribute it to my good humour at discovering the tractor – and Drew – escaped any real damage in yesterday's mishap, or you can attribute it to causes unknown. Very well, then, we have a date."

And he got up and went off to work, whistling cheerfully. I sat where I was for a few minutes, thinking. I had said: 'I'd like to go'. And I felt, oddly, that I had meant it.

Why had I? I was no gambler, though I found it absorbing to watch other people gambling. Had I meant I would like to go out with Tony? I frowned, wanting instantly to deny that, yet knowing that I had to admit to myself that, imposter though I knew him to be, Tony carried with him an air of excitement which I could never define.

From a purely practical viewpoint, I told myself, it would give me a revealing insight into Tony's character. There was about him, about the very situation he was placed in, the touch of the gambling instinct. I had often wondered, when he went out alone at night as he occasionally did, without any hint to where he was going, whether he went to the casino, drawn by a compulsion to gamble.

Tonight I would find out.

The casino in its riverside setting was fairly crowded, and buzzed with chatter and laughter as people set about trying their luck at the tables. There was an unmistakable air of excitement which I reflected wouldn't be found anywhere else. No matter how much any of these people would protest that this was a fun thing, just another night out, the fact remained that everyone present had at least a little dream – the dream of one of those fantastic runs of luck which do sometimes – just sometimes – happen. Who could say it wouldn't happen tonight? And if it did, who knew to whom it would happen?

I had to admit to myself that I was not immune from the fever, either.

I was content to watch while Tony tried his hand fairly briefly at chemin de fer, a game which was outside my threadbare gambling knowledge. He lost, but not much.

He looked up at me. "Going to try your hand?"

I shook my head. "I'll stick to roulette. It's the thing that's intrigued me the very few times I had my small flutter at casinos."

"Well, we'll move to the roulette tables, then, if that's what you enjoy."

"It's not the game itself so much that interests me," I explained. "It's the people. To see them so absorbed in the turn of a wheel – it's fascinating, but it's a little frightening, too."

"Frightening?" He raised his eyebrows and laughed. "What a funny girl you are. Come, let's try our luck."

The tables were crowded, but we finally took our places. "I'm starting with five dollars," I had told Tony firmly when we bought our chips. "When I lose that I'm quitting."

He grinned in huge amusement. "Well, that shouldn't be too frightening a financial loss," he conceded. "What then?"

"I'll be content just to watch," I assured him.

He shrugged. "Tell you what, be a devil just this once and play ten dollars. I'll shout you the other five."

He did, and I watched carefully, while trying to appear not to watch at all, to see how much he would begin with. He changed fifty dollars into chips, and while I wasn't willing to toss that much into the waiting coffers of any casino, I had to admit to myself that if he gambled only occasionally fifty dollars was hardly wild excess, if he left it at that.

I managed to lose my ten dollars rather quickly and retired from the table to stand back and watch Tony.

He played with a glitter of excitement in his eyes, but another half hour sufficed to tell me that, while he greatly enjoyed the element of risk, he was no compulsive gambler. If Fairfield ever became his, he wouldn't lose it at the tables of a casino. I let my attention wander to the other players.

Most people were there for fun and a mild flutter, and their stakes usually ranged somewhere between Tony's and mine.

But there were others.

Others for whom this was a drug, a necessity; something they were hooked on as much as if they were mainlining heroin. There was a plump, jolly little man in evening dress who joked gaily whether he won or lost, and only the clenching and unclenching of his hands betrayed the terrible need to win. A tall, grey-haired man in a blue lounge-suit smoked a cigar and played in silent absorption, not caring if the whole world knew his weakness – not even aware the rest of the world existed. He won nearly three thousand dollars while I watched, and his expression never changed.

A blonde woman in an elegant gown, a silver-fox cape flung around her shoulders with the casualness of custom, laughed and chatted to her escort, but her eyes were feverishly bright and a pulse in her throat told she was under fierce tension. She was losing. Badly. Anyone who only heard her voice could well have believed it didn't matter.

Tony's small fortunes fluctuated. When he was about twenty dollars ahead, after having been forty down, he looked around at me and smiled. "Time to relax," he said, stepping away from the table. "Let's have a drink."

He seemed to be known in the casino, at least to some of the staff. The man who served our drinks, a slight dark man with deft hands and a European accent, called him 'Mr Maynard.'

"Jake," Tony said, "the lady just likes to watch the people rather than play. What do you think of that?"

He smiled. "It is fortunate not all our patrons are like that. But mam'selle is wise, perhaps. I have worked in casinos in Europe many years, mam'selle, and I assure you it is the wise who do not play."

"But the adventurous do, eh, Jake?" Tony said.

"That, m'sieu, yes."

"Miss Baker has been watching the people at the roulette. The lady in the blue dress and the fur cape is losing. A lot. Can she afford to?"

Jake shrugged. "She is here often," he said, as if that covered everything.

Tony laughed. "Jake, the soul of discretion, eh? You keep the fortunes of the customers a secret."

Jake spread his hands. "I do not know their fortunes, Mr Maynard. They play, and sometimes they win and sometimes they do not. Me, I serve drinks. I do not see their bank account statements."

"Jake," I said slowly, "can anyone beat the wheel?"

"Ah, but sometimes a player can win much, much money, mam'selle. Oh, yes."

"But I mean, is there such a thing as a system in gambling – any form of gambling, not just roulette? A real system?"

He suddenly smiled a flash of excellent teeth. "There are many systems, mam'selle. If there was one which worked I would not work at the casino. I would own it." And he moved smoothly away.

Tony and I had an excellent supper, and as we drove home we discussed the people we had seen, and the whole business of gambling, and our conversation was lively and stimulating. Tony had a quick mind, and while he didn't share my sense of near-sadness over the people who were caught in the gamblers' trap – 'We're all free agents, Anne, and whatever situation of that kind people may get into, it's by their own choice of a line of action' – he, too, was impressed and intrigued by the power that could be exerted over a person's life by something so elementally upredictable as the spin of a wheel.

He stopped the car in the drive before the front door, and as I gathered up my evening shawl and handbag he said quietly, "Anne."

I turned and looked at him enquiringly, thinking somewhere toward the back of my mind how devastatingly handsome he was in dinner jacket and black tie. He just sat for a moment looking at me, as if for once he had nothing to say.

Then he said softly, "Damn!" And he pulled me quickly but not roughly against him, his mouth finding mine hungrily and compellingly. To what would have been my surprise if I had been capable of intelligent thought at that moment, I let my shawl slip from my shoulders as my arms went around his neck and I returned his kiss.

Somewhere in the depths of my brain I finally heard the warning bell which told me this was dangerous madness, and I pulled away from him. "No!" I said sharply.

"But why? Anne –"

"Because it's impossible – it would be an impossible situation. You know that as well as I do. I work here."

I took a quick breath. "It's been a grand evening, Tony. Don't let's spoil it."

I quickly picked up my shawl and handbag again and turned to open the car door. He reached swiftly across to catch my wrist, saying, "Anne, wait! I'm not –"

He accidentally knocked my handbag from my grasp and it fell on the floor of the car and snapped open to spill its contents on the floor.

At once he bent apologetically to pick up the things for me. "Sorry, I didn't mean to be a clumsy oaf. And I wouldn't want to do anything to spoil your evening, because I hope you might let me take you out again. Thank you for coming tonight. There, I think that's everything, though I must confess the contents of women's purses baffle me. Oh, hang on, there's something else fallen under the seat."

To my horror I saw too late what it was, and that it had fallen revealingly open.

"Hello, it's your driving licence. Do you always carry it, or did you think I'd get tanked and you'd have to drive home?"

I had put my passport in a Hobart Bank safe-deposit box, but I had to keep my British driving licence available.

I held out my hand for it as casually as I could. "Force of habit, I suppose," I said.

I hoped desperately that my voice sounded unconcerned. The light from the car's interior light, which he had fiicked on to aid in the search for my spilled possessions, even combined with the light from the dashboard, was very soft and the licence wouldn't be too easy to read.

He glanced at it idly and proceeded to read the description of me. "Height – hmm. Hair – hmm. Eyes – green. Yes, I suppose they are."

He smiled and began to hand the licence to me, and then

suddenly he froze.

I don't suppose it was for more than a few seconds that we sat like a pair of statues, but it seemed a very long time.

Finally Tony leaned back and looked at me. "Well, well," he said softly. "The prim little Miss Baker has a secret life!"

For a moment still hopeful that he wouldn't attach any particular importance to the name on the licence, I said shortly, "If I choose to use another name, it's really none of your business, is it?"

"Oh, but it is, my love, it is. I engaged you to care for my elderly and helpless grandmother. I have a right to know just who it is I've hired, haven't I?"

He looked back at the licence. "Anne Elizabeth Beaconsfield." He frowned. "Beaconsfield. Anne Beaconsfield. Now where have I –" He stopped as the realization hit him, and presently, very slowly, he turned his head to look at me again, his voice and eyes dangerous.

"So," he said, and the tone was velvet over the edge of a sword. "And what game are you playing, Miss Beaconsfield?"

"I might," I retorted coldly, "ask you the same question."

"Then why didn't you ask it in the first place?" He hadn't moved, but somehow he seemed suddenly to tower over me. "Why *haven't* you asked it, eh? That first day, in the store, when you saw me – why didn't you shout fraud and police?"

The controlled fury in his tone made it seem absurdly as if our positions were reversed, and I was the true imposter on Fairfield.

"Because, Mr Robert Harrison, the postmistress had just told me how dangerous my grandmother's heart condition was. And she *was* my grandmother, even though she was a total stranger. I wasn't prepared to expose her to the shock of learning that the nice young man she believed to be her grandson was a fraud engaged in Heaven alone knew what kind of nastiness. I had to make a very quick decision, and I made it. I stayed to protect her interests where I could. The circumstances basically haven't changed. I still haven't felt it was safe to risk the shock of the truth."

Tony sat for a little time in silence, looking down at the driving licence in his hands. Presently he handed it back to me, and the anger seemed to have drained out of him.

"I see," he said slowly. "And how do you think I came to be posing as Tony Maynard? It wouldn't occur to you that I had a small glimmer of humanity, too, would it?"

"You could," I said, "try surprising me."

"My dear girl, it was out of consideration for the old lady – misplaced consideration, wrong judgment though it may have been – that I got myself entangled in this business in the first place. I didn't set out to deceive her. It just happened that I was caught up in the situation before I knew what was happening. You wouldn't believe me if I told you the truth, would you?"

"Miracles happen," I said drily.

"You know about the accident that happened on our way here, when supposedly Bob Harrison was killed?"

"Yes."

"Then it must have occurred to you to wonder how the mistaken identity ever happened."

"Drew Thomas told me you had a letter on you – a letter from Mrs Maynard to Tony – and I presume the logical assumption anyone would make, on going through your pockets in search of identification when you were taken to hospital, was that you were Tony. You seem to have done very little, to put it mildly, to dispel the illusion. It was very convenient for you that you didn't happen to have any papers of your own on you."

"There's a very simple explanation – one of those freaks of chance which happen easily enough, but only *matter* once in a thousand times to get noticed. Apparently on the night of the accident, Tony and I had got our wallets mixed. It had happened before, because the wallets were identical, and it had become a bit of a joke between us. The night of the accident we'd stopped to have dinner at a little pub, and we'd both had our wallets out on the table while we settled the check. When we got up from the table we must have picked up the wrong wallets. We'd been talking about whether we'd stay there for the night or push on a bit farther. Tony was keen to go on, and I wasn't tired, so we decided to keep going for a bit. I was driving."

He paused for a moment.

"Any blame there is for what happened has to rest on me, I guess. All I remember is lights suddenly in my face on a bend in the road as a car came around much too wide. I swung the wheel to avoid a head-on, and the rest is mercifully a blur of half-remembered things and quite a few complete blanks. But when I first came to in hospital *everything* was blank. I'd had some concussion, apparently, and I had temporary amnesia. I didn't know where I was or who I was or where I'd come from. They were calling me Mr Maynard, so I supposed that was my name.

"They brought Mrs Maynard in – because her letter, with her name and address was in Tony's wallet in my trouser-pocket, along with his driving licence and his birth certificate. She was so glad to see me and know I was still alive that I was very touched, and I might add that it was a rather good feeling at that moment to have someone who cared about me. The old lady was so happy about me that when my memory came back a few hours later I simply didn't have the heart to tell her that her grandson was dead.

"I thought I could break the news later, or tell the doctor or the police and they could do it for me. But I found out about her heart condition and I couldn't do it. I mean, if she could have been told in the first place that Tony was dead, when he was still only a name to her, she could have taken it. But to find out the fellow she thought was her grandson, and had been so delighted to see, was just his companion, and Tony had died in the smash – well, that was very different. I kept thinking the opportunity to tell the truth would come along, but it just grew more impossible."

He flicked a glance at me. "So I took up the role of being someone else – just as you did, and for just the same reasons. Using the signature on Tony's driving licence for a model, I learned to copy that, and his general style of writing. I'd known him long enough, and knew enough about his background, to be convincing. And I've tried very hard never to be too disappointing a grandson."

"Touching," I said shortly. "Also very advantageous to Mr Bob Harrison."

"I've worked damned hard for everything I've got!"

"And everything you hope to get."

There was a little pause, and then he shrugged. "That's true enough. I'm a practical man. Tony's dead. Nothing can change that. Sure, I'm happy there's something in it for me. But you wouldn't have begrudged Tony his share of his grandmother's estate. Well, instead of the death of the only remaining member of her family she had contact with, I've given her a grandson – given a lonely old lady someone to care about, a feeling of family again. Is it so unreasonable to be willing to accept a reward for that?"

I didn't answer for a moment, and he went on quietly:

"You think I'm a swine, probably a criminal one. But, Anne, what would you have had me do? You yourself chose to hold your tongue about me rather than risk a shock that might kill her. What was I supposed to do in that position? Can you tell me?"

"If you'd spoken up in the first place, when your memory first came back, I hardly think the shock would have been too great," I said.

"You're probably right. But I didn't. And remember I was a shade battered myself, and not thinking awfully clearly. I drifted into the situation. I didn't set out to cheat the old lady and I don't really feel I have. You've known her for long enough, Anne: don't you think she's a good deal happier with me around the place than without anyone?"

I remembered Mrs Maynard saying softly as she had looked out over the garden and the orchard frothy with blossom on a bright spring morning: 'I would have been forced to give it up, if Tony hadn't come. It's like seeing our family line regenerated, given another chance.'

I looked at him helplessly. "Yes," I said.

"Then is it such a bad thing I'm doing? Who am I really cheating?"

I didn't answer, and Tony said:

"Oh Lord yes, I see. Of course. There's you. I haven't got used to the idea that you're a member of the family. But it's very probable, don't you think, that none of this makes the least difference to what you would have inherited, anyway. And Anne."

"Yes?"

"Correct me if I'm wrong, but I don't think you came here for the purpose of making sure you picked up a good share of your grandmother's small fortune."

"Hardly," I said curtly, "since for all I knew she was penniless."

He nodded. "You've grown fond of her, haven't you?"

"Yes, I have."

"Certainly she's fond of you. So there really isn't anything much either of us can do about the status quo, is there?"

I stared. "Are you saying you want me to just – just be a party to this?"

"Mrs Maynard's health hasn't been changed by anything you and I know about each other." There was a momentary flash of anger in his eyes and in his voice. "I don't suppose it has occurred to you that *I* might have grown to care about her, too, has it?"

Then he added more quietly, "Please, Anne, while she lives, let it ride. All right, after that, if you choose you can blow my cover sky-high. That's my bad luck. I warn you I'll try very hard to persuade you in the meantime to let me get away with it, but in the end it will be up to you."

"You were pretty determined to strengthen your position when you brought Glenda Forbes out here," I pointed out.

He rubbed his chin. "What seemed like a sound move when I made it, doesn't look such a happy thought now, perhaps, but Glenda was the only person I had in the world, the one person I could trust absolutely. And it seemed to me that if I was going to have a secure way of life, she had the right to share it. Her name is Forbes, all right, because she married a fellow named Forbes who had the decency to get himself killed six months later by falling under a train while in his normal state of drunken imbecility. Glenda's not any ex-girlfriend. She's my sister."

I gaped at him, dumbfounded.

He made an impatient movement. "She hasn't had the easiest of lives, one way and another. She went to Canada when her husband was killed. She lost her job there a few months ago and went back to England, but she found it very hard to get work there, too, so I suggested she come out here. We've kept in touch, incidentally, by way of a post office box in Hobart where she sent all my letters, and I collected them whenever I went to town. She couldn't come out here as my sister, since Tony Maynard had no sister, so the alternative was that she could come as an old friend."

At least some of the things which had seemed to me rather odd about their relationship now fell into place.

"I see," was all I could think of saying.

Tony sat, not looking at me. Presently he said, "Anne."

"Yes?"

"When Anne Beaconsfield was a shadowy figure – just a name on the other side of the world who meant nothing to her grandmother, I quite frankly didn't in the least care if Grandma left every cent to me and dropped Anne completely out of her will. I'll be honest about that. I never set out to cheat anyone and I didn't *wish* to cheat anyone. But I didn't feel I was cheating Anne Beaconsfield of anything. Fate dropped me into a position where Bob Harrison, out-of-work motor-mechanic who'd never really had a bean in his life, had a golden opportunity to be comfortably off for the rest of his days. I reckoned that if Margaret Maynard got to like me well enough to leave me Fairfield Orchard, I was going to grab that chance with both hands and reckon I'd earned it.

"But now – well, you're here. You came because of your grandmother, and she's grown fond of you. It – it's different."

"Nice of you to notice," I said.

"Please don't be sarcastic. Suddenly it all seems – just a rather sordid mess."

"I'm sure your agile brain will think of a very logical means of resolving the situation," I told him.

"I can't resolve it," he said. "You hold the trump card. You can quite successfully challenge Grandma's will by exposing me as an imposter. I'll be disinherited and quite possibly will do a bit of a term in jail. But can I ask you one thing?"

"I've no doubt you will, anyway. What is it?"

"Remembering the work I've done on Fairfield and the fact I've brought your grandmother some happiness, do you think I've earned the right to some place in her affections, and perhaps some consideration in the sharing out of her estate?"

I turned my head and looked at him. "Yes," I said after a while. "I guess you have. Perhaps a good deal more than I have. Now if you don't mind, I'm too weary to think any more. We have no choice but to carry on as if nothing had happened. So for the moment, please leave it. Goodnight."

I got out of the car and went into the house. As I went through to my room I heard him start the car and drive it around to the garage. I wondered if Mrs Gootch, who had come over to sleep in a spare room so that Mrs Maynard would not be alone in the house, had heard the car come and wondered at the long delay before I came into the house.

I undressed and got into bed. I had said I was too weary

to think, but I was also too full of thoughts to sleep. But through the maze of thoughts entangled in my brain I kept coming back to one thing: in the final analysis, Fairfield and anything else Mrs Maynard may own were hers to bequeath as she chose. And if she chose to leave Fairfield to Bob Harrison, was she not in fact leaving it to the man she knew and loved, the man she wanted to own it, not simply leaving it on principle to a grandson?

I would have every legal right in the world to intervene. But had I any *moral* right?

I shook my pillow into a new shape for perhaps the tenth time and tried to relax. It occurred to me that the one thing which had puzzled me from the beginning – how Tony planned to convince the authorities of his Anthony Maynard identity in order to collect any inheritance – had perhaps been answered.

He had said that among other papers in the real Tony's wallet, which had been inadvertently switched with his, had been Tony's birth certificate and driving licence. That, I thought, might well be regarded as sufficient proof of identity. All their other papers, passports and so on, would have been destroyed in the fire when the car burned.

Fate, as Tony had said, had dropped him into an imposter's role which had indeed been easy enough for an adventurous spirit to accept without any real feeling of wrong-doing. Even I could see that. And was there any real wrong-doing anyway?

I turned restlessly. I had no need to make any decision yet as to whether or not I exposed Tony as a fraud. For the present, as long as my grandmother lived, I had no choice but to go along as before. I was Anne Baker, housekeeper-companion, and the fair-haired man who had taken me out to the casino only a few hours ago was Tony Maynard, Margaret Maynard's grandson. Nothing had really changed.

And I knew that was not true.

The relationship between Tony and me had changed,

now that he knew who I was and what I knew of him. I refused to consider whether our relationship had changed in another way also. Refused to try to analyse what my feelings had been in those moments when he had held me crushed against him, and, my arms around his neck, I had kissed him and wanted him. I had, I told myself firmly, far too many things on my mind to give that brief incident breathing-room. But the memory was not easy to shut out.

Ten

Glenda Forbes came back two days before Christmas and Tony went into Hobart in his own car to pick her up from the tourist-coach terminus. Neither of us had spoken of the night we had been to the casino. Tony behaved, even when we were alone together, exactly as if it had never happened, and I accepted that that was the only course to take. To play our character roles in public and revert to our real positions in private would have placed an intolerable strain on us both.

I was doing some weeding in the garden when Tony and Glenda arrived, and presently Glenda came out to where I was working.

She was a little pale, and she looked at me with anxious eyes. "Tony's told me, of course, that you know about us," she said.

I sat back on my heels and looked at her.

"Anne, you must think Tony is some kind of criminal, I guess – a confidence trickster at the best. But he isn't like that, truly he isn't. He's always been the kind to do crazy things – dangerous things like mountain-climbing and parachute-jumping – things that would scare me to death. He went to the Isle of Skye once for a holiday and went climbing alone in the Cuillens, without telling anyone, in weather when no one in his right senses would have done it, and he was stranded for three days because the weather closed in."

She was looking at me intently, as if begging me to see this man as she saw him.

"He's the kind of man who thrives on danger, Anne. But it's always been – well, danger to himself, not to anyone else. Do you see what I mean? When he came to his senses after the accident and found everyone believed he was Tony Maynard, when the idea had time to really register, he got excited about it. It was like climbing a mountain in a storm, I guess. If he fell – well, *he* was the one who was going to get hurt. And if he succeeded in being Tony Maynard, he still wasn't hurting anyone. Until he knew about you, of course," she added.

"Our home life wasn't much. Our parents constantly fought, and drank, and ended up by each clearing off with someone else – oh, not until Bob – sorry, I mustn't do that: I mean Tony – was eighteen and I was sixteen. But I'd have been out on a pretty unpleasant limb if it hadn't been for Tony. He stuck by me and looked after me – kept us both on his apprentice's wages until I could leave school and get a job. We didn't exactly live in luxury, but we scraped by. And it's always been like that. He might do daft things, but he's always been there to make sure I was all right.

"I was in Canada and had a pretty good job when Tony Maynard suggested they might both migrate to Australia because he had a grandmother here with a valuable property and no-one to leave it to. Oh, Bob – my Tony – said Tony Maynard did tell him he had a cousin somewhere, but she didn't count because nobody knew where she was and she'd never kept in touch with her grandmother."

She looked at me uneasily as if she expected some kind of denial of this.

"That's true enough," I said. "My father wasn't ever much of a correspondent, and of course my mother's mother was really a stranger to him and he kept only the sketchiest of letter-contact with her. And when he died, I simply didn't know my grandmother's address – only the name of the village stuck in my mind – and at the age I was then, an elderly grandmother on the other side of the world, and whom you've never seen, assumes little importance in your mind."

I felt a flash of annoyance with myself. Why was I explaining myself to Glenda Forbes?

I said abruptly, "Did you know my cousin Tony?"

"I'd met him," Glenda said. "I didn't like him very much. I wished he and B – Tony weren't friends."

"Why?"

Interest in her remark probably sharpened my tone, because she looked uncomfortable.

"I don't really know," she said. "I felt he and my Tony were bad for each other. I'm not sure – I don't think I can explain how. It was – well, once we had two lots of neighbours who each had a dog. On their own, they were quite well-behaved dogs, but when they got together they'd chase cats and bail up the postman."

I was silent for a minute. I had a feeling that perhaps Glenda Forbes, whom I wouldn't have put down as being the most astute of people, had just made a very significant comment.

When I didn't say anything Glenda added, "Tony isn't bad, Anne, truly he isn't."

"You mean that left to his own devices he doesn't chase cats or bail up the postman," I said drily.

"He's worked awfully hard here, and he and Mrs Maynard are really very fond of each other. What – what are you going to do about him?"

"For the moment, nothing," I said. "In the end – I don't know, Glenda. To be perfectly honest, I have no idea."

I went back to my weeding. Glenda stood for a minute and then turned and walked away. I felt a twinge of pity for her. Tony was her hero. Evidently he had always been good to her, helped and protected her. The result was that whatever Tony did would be right in Glenda's eyes. He was the strong one, the decisive one. What happened to *her* would always be of secondary importance to Glenda. What happened to Tony would always be paramount.

I jabbed viciously with the hand-fork at the roots of offending weeds. There was a strange aching lump inside me and unshed tears stung behind my eyes.

I had lied when I told Glenda I didn't know what I was going to do about Tony. Even as I said it I had believed it, but I knew now that it wasn't true. I did know what I was going to do.

The realization struck me with the force of a slap in the face. I didn't know how long I'd known what I was going to do, but I did know.

I was going to do precisely nothing.

When the time came, when Margaret Maynard died, I would leave Fairfield Orchard as Anne Baker, at once and without telling anyone. Anne Beaconsfield could reappear in Sydney or anywhere else. Whatever my grandmother chose to do with her property could stand. I couldn't make the decision over whether or not Robert Harrison, imposter, had any rights. So I would take what was probably the coward's course and run away.

Why that decision should hurt so dreadfully I wasn't sure and I refused to analyse it. I only knew that it had nothing to do with money. It was something much more important than that.

Christmas Day was brightly sunny, but a pleasant breeze stopped it from being too hot. Mrs Maynard called me to her room early and said she was feeling very well and would like to go to Church, so I drove her to attend a seven o'clock service in the local Church, packed with people, mainly orchardists, who knew her and were plainly delighted to see her.

The Gootches had their own family plans for the day, so

Mrs Maynard's guests were Drew and his parents, whom I hadn't met before and whom I immediately liked, and Ashley Maclean and his mother, who arrived just before the meal was ready. I hadn't seen Ashley since the day of the tractor accident. He had telephoned twice to ask me out, once to dinner and once to a stage show in Hobart, but each time I had made an excuse.

I had not been looking forward to this day when he and Drew would have to sit down at the same table, Drew believing Ashley may well have tried to kill him; both of us knowing he may well have killed Janet Chisholm.

Drew carried it off with all the poise that could have been expected of a mature adult. He made no attempt to avoid Ashley, and no one who didn't know the situation could possibly have suspected anything wrong. But a couple of times during dinner I saw him watching Ashley with troubled eyes, a tense, grim set about his mouth. Ashley, for his part, seemed perfectly unconstrained and relaxed. If there was anything significant in the way he looked or spoke to Drew, I couldn't detect it.

Ashley's mother was a tall woman – a little stooped now, but she must once have been as tall as Ashley. She was very thin and had the laboured breathing of the chronic asthmatic, and she spent most of her time in a wheelchair, but her brown eyes were alert and she spoke to me warmly.

"Anne – I may call you Anne, mayn't I? – I'm so glad to meet you. Ashley has told me about you. You're English. Tell me, do you feel a little homesick for an English Christmas?"

I smiled. "Not really. I haven't any family in England now, and from what I've heard of the winter they've been having this year I think I'm lucky to be here in the sunshine."

We chattered comfortably. She was a gentle, gracious woman with a sense of humour, and I liked her immediately. And, liking her, I was filled with a dull feeling of cold sickness. Ashley would have to be an insensitive man indeed not to be filled with rage if Janet Chisholm had threatened to spread to this woman's ears the rumour – however false – that her son had cruelly killed his father and brother.

It was a Christmas Day I didn't enjoy, even though it was certainly one I would never forget. So many emotional undercurrents were running among the people who gathered at that dinner-table that it seemed to me as if a cloud of gas hung in the room, undetectable, and a single careless or unknowing spark could explode it.

But the spark was not lit. Everything went smoothly. Tony, handsome and good-humoured, was the perfect host; Glenda the helpful and appreciative house-guest. Drew was his normal chatting, lively self. Ashley, with his innate courtesy and slow smile, was relaxed, utterly likeable. It was one of Mrs Maynard's good days as far as her health was concerned, and she was animated and obviously enjoyed herself.

And I somehow managed to get through the day. All my thinking was dominated by the feeling that the present situation could not and would not go on. It was too highly-charged, too explosive. Something, somewhere, was going to happen.

Glenda helped me clear away after dinner and wash the dishes while the others relaxed and chatted in the cool of the wide verandah. Then she went back to join the others and I, feeling suddenly that I must be alone for a while, went out into the garden and sat on a wooden garden-seat in the shade of one of the elms. Out of sight of the others on the verandah and out of hearing of everything except an occasional sound of laughter, I leaned back and closed my eyes, feeling terribly weary and as if I never wanted to be bothered with thinking again.

"Anne."

I started violently, my momentary illusion of peace shattered.

"I'm sorry," Ashley said. "You're tired. I shouldn't have

disturbed you."

He came across the lawn and sat down beside me. "I came to tell you I must go now and take Mother back. She's very tired, but she has so much enjoyed the day." He smiled at me. "She likes you."

"I like her," I said candidly. "I'm very glad she was well enough to come."

"She'd like you to visit her sometimes when you're in Hobart and you have the time. Would you?"

"Of course." I said it mechanically. I didn't add: While I'm here.

"Thank you, Anne. I'd like to drive you down to Port Arthur one day. We can have lunch there and look over the ruins of the convict settlement and –"

"No!" I said. "No – thank you."

He looked at me with a slightly startled expression and I realized I'd spoken with sharp emphasis.

"I'm sorry," I said hastily. "I'm sure it would be very interesting, but I wouldn't want to leave Mrs Maynard for a whole day like that. She shouldn't be left for long alone."

There was a little silence. Ashley picked up a fallen elm leaf and seemed absorbed in a study of its structure. "I see," he said presently. "Suppose you tell me the real reason?"

"But I told you. Mrs Maynard hasn't been so well, and –"

"Anne." He didn't raise his voice, but it cut mine to silence. "This friend of Tony's – Glenda – can keep an eye on Mrs Maynard for a few hours, plus which Mrs Maynard is in fact looking extremely well, for her. Please don't lie to me. You don't want to go out with me."

It was a statement, not a question, and I made no answer.

"I wish you would tell me why. You went out with me several times and I thought you and I enjoyed each other's company. Now suddenly it's as if I have something rather nasty which may be contagious. Why?"

"Why?" he repeated.

I still didn't answer and he reached out quickly to grab my wrist. Utterly without thinking I leapt to my feet and backed away from him.

He sat staring at me, horror in his eyes. "Oh, my God," he said softly.

Devastatingly, I was afraid of him, and he realized it.

When I could force myself to think of something to say I stammered, "I'll go – go up to the house and say goodbye to your mother. She – must be tired. I'm so glad she could come."

I turned and began to walk toward the house, feeling suddenly that it was a long way.

"Anne."

I stopped without looking back, but I knew he hadn't moved. I wasn't quite sure why I'd even stopped, since there was nothing in the world I wanted so much as to end this scene; but there was something in his voice which made it somehow necessary to listen, perhaps even answer the question I knew must come.

"What is it that you've heard about me?"

My mind answered: Enough to hang you, if they still hang murderers in this state. Aloud I said, "Leave it, please, Ashley."

"No, I will not leave it." I knew he had stood up, and I heard his footsteps stop close behind me. "You've always known – you must have been told at the beginning – that as far as the police are concerned I have to be prime suspect in Janet Chisholm's murder. The crime of passion. You knew that, didn't you?"

"Yes." My voice wasn't entirely steady.

"You knew it, and you went out with me – alone, and more than once. So I can only assume that you didn't believe it. What's happened, Anne? What happened to make you change your mind? Someone has said something. What?"

His voice was still quiet, but there was a violent

undercurrent in it.

"Ashley, I said leave it."

"And I said I will not!" He grabbed me by the shoulders and spun me around to face him. The grey-blue eyes were no longer dreamy, and there was no slow smile hovering about the sensitive mouth. Cold rage filled every fibre of him. I had the sudden thought that this was the way Janet Chisholm must have seen him the day she had threatened him with blackmail. Probably no-one else but Janet had ever seen the quietly charming Ashley Maclean look the way he was looking at me now.

Perhaps Janet had seen that same look the night she had died – if in fact she had seen her murderer at all before she was struck down from behind.

"What have you heard?" His hands were clamped bruisingly on my shoulders. "What has someone said to you? *What*?"

I said, before I knew I was going to tell him, "You were seen next morning. After Janet was killed. With clothes – your clothes – with blood on them."

For what may have been a full minute he stood utterly immobile, his hands still gripped on my shoulders. In the silence, somewhere in the distance I heard a crow caw lazily, and from the verandah of Fairfield came the sound of a woman's laugh. I think it was Glenda's.

Ashley said slowly, "I see." He looked at his hands on my shoulders almost as if they didn't belong to him, and at once released me.

He said, "Why didn't whoever saw me tell the police?"

"Because that person didn't want the responsibility of perhaps getting you arrested while there was any chance it might all be some mistake – just a fearful coincidence."

There was a pause, and then he said, "It seems I am much indebted to an unknown admirer." There was a flick of cycnicism in his tone. "But you don't believe in any such fearful coincidence."

It wasn't exactly a question, but, off-guard, I said,

"There have been other things."

What he saw in my face I have no idea. Abruptly he turned away. "I must go," he said. "My mother will be too tired."

I walked to the house with him in silence, feeling like a space-traveller returning from some strange fearsome planet and finding the earth no less a nightmare than the place he has left behind.

But even though I was only the housekeeper at Fairfield, Mrs Maynard's lack of strength placed some degree of duty as hostess on me, and common courtesy demanded I should be there to bid goodbye to the guests, and especially to Mrs Maclean. Ashley and Tony helped her into the car, and she extracted a promise from me to visit her.

Mrs Maynard said she must rest also, and excused herself from the group on the verandah. I went with her to her room to make sure she was comfortable, and she looked at me keenly.

"You don't look well, Anne. Have you been working too hard?"

I smiled. "No, of course not. Just a headache. Have you enjoyed the day?"

"Very much. You're a good hostess, Anne. Thank you. Tell me, did you like Drew's parents? And Ashley's mother?"

"Very much."

"Good." She shook her head. "So sad to see Ashley's mother as ill as she is. So much younger than I am and even more an invalid. I wonder sometimes whether she would have been like that if her husband and son hadn't been killed. Tragedy can so much affect the body as well as the mind. Sometimes when Ashley looks at his mother I suspect he is thinking much the same thing."

"Yes," I said. "I expect perhaps he is."

Eleven

A few days after New Year, Lesleigh Martin and I played nine holes of golf together, as we occasionally did. I took my car and picked Lesleigh up at the Martin house, and as we were leaving she asked if I would stop at their roadside mailbox to pick up their mail. She put the letters, unopened, on the parcel shelf of the car, and it was only when I arrived home after dropping Lesleigh at her place after our game that I discovered she had forgotten the letters.

I hadn't time to drive over and return them then, as it was time to get the dinner under way, so I made a mental note to deliver them later in the evening. I announced at the dinner-table that I would walk over to the Martins' place after I'd done the dishes, and return the letters.

Drew, after spending the week from Christmas to New Year with his parents, had come back to the orchard, and he at once offered to take the mail.

I shook my head. "Thanks, Drew, but I'll enjoy it, truly. It's a beautiful evening, just pleasantly cool after the heat today, and there's a moon that's half-way to full. It'll be lovely to walk the short-cut by the forest track."

The so-called forest track was really a link-up of tractor-trails, first through Fairfield, then across the edge of Ashley Maclean's orchard – not near his house – along a track through an arm of pine forest which belonged to Oakhill, across a wooden bridge over a stream that ran through the forest, and then through the Martins' orchard.

"Good gracious, girl," Mrs Maynard said, "why ever

don't you take the car? I don't like the idea of you being out walking alone at night."

"I'll go with you," Drew volunteered.

I laughed. "Nonsense! The chances of coming to any harm on that track would be about equal to the chances of being hit by a meteorite. It's not much more than a kilometre each way, and I love to walk in the moonlight. We all use cars too much. You never see the world by moonlight at all if you're in a car."

I was glad I had chosen to walk. The night was perfectly clear and the moonlight lay brilliantly silver over the orchards. Already the fruit on the trees was almost fully developed and in just a few weeks picking would begin in a flurry of activity, but on this night utter peace seemed to reign.

There was only a light breeze, and my footsteps were muffled on the turf of the orchards, so that the only sound was the softly-rounded notes of a pair of owls calling to each other, and the occasional distant sound of a car passing along the road.

I walked, drinking in the beauty and the tranquillity of the world transformed from all the colours of daylight to this simple black-and-silver, and I shut my mind against tormenting thoughts, and was almost at peace.

The heavy shadows of the pine forest made me wish I had brought a torch, but the track was smooth enough and I walked carefully, and even in the shadow there was some sprinkling of dappled moonlight. I stopped for a minute on the sturdy little wooden bridge and listened to the rippling of the stream and drank in the clear, tangy scent of pine-needles. Just below the bridge the stream widened and deepened into a fair-sized pool. I wondered briefly if there were trout here; I must remember to ask someone – not that I was in any way a fisherman.

At the Martins' I found Lesleigh and her two brothers playing Mah Jong, and they welcomed me cheerfully and invited me to join them. Patrick, a year or two older than

Lesleigh, was dark and quiet; Evan, just turned twenty-one, had Lesleigh's copper-red hair and was effervescently talkative. They all seemed to have an excellent relationship, arguing and trading insults with a casual lightheartedness which indicated they got on very well together. I wondered whether Lesleigh's brothers knew or guessed her drug problem. I suspected not.

The phone rang while we were playing and Patrick said to Evan: "Better answer it. It'll be one of your multitude of girlfriends. To avoid embarrassment, bear in mind that we can't help hearing every word you say."

Since the telephone was in the livingroom where we were playing, that was perfectly true, even though, since we had to suspend play while Evan was away from the table, Lesleigh and I began to chat about golf and Patrick, who also played a little, joined in.

The telephone caller was Ashley, on some orchard business, and presently Evan excused himself and said he would have to cut the conversation short.

"We're playing Mah Jong and I don't want to hold the game up, because Anne's here – walked over from Fairfield and insists she's going to walk back because she likes the moonlight, would you believe. So we mustn't keep her too late."

When we had played some four or five games Lesleigh made coffee and I set out to walk home, brushing aside their repeated offers to drive me.

"No way," I smiled. "I enjoyed the walk over too much to miss the chance to repeat it. Thank you for the evening – it was fun."

It had been. The Martins were good company. I felt more relaxed and lighthearted than I had for weeks. The air was much cooler than when I had walked over, but it was no more than pleasantly crisp, and the moonlight, once my eyes adjusted to it after coming from the lighted house, was just as brilliant, even though the moon had slipped toward the western horizon. The owls had stopped calling to each other, and even the intermittent traffic out on the road seemed to have stopped for the night. It was so quiet I could hear the occasional rustle of some tiny creature of the night – a field mouse or possibly a bandicoot – as it scurried off into the grass at the verge of the planted section of the orchard, alarmed by my footfalls. Once I heard the click and scrape of a possum's claws as it scrambled up an apple tree and, pausing, I could see it in the moonlight, sitting on a branch watching me more in curiosity than concern. I smiled to myself and walked on.

I was still in the Martins' orchard, almost at the point where it joined Ashley Maclean's, when I first began to think I was being followed.

The uneasiness came to me slowly, nebulously, at first little more than a kind of instinct, a queer prickling sensation down my spine. I told myself it was a trick of my imagination brought on by the fact everyone had been offering to drive me, and sharpened by the solitary feeling of being wakeful in a world where my fellow-creatures were sleeping.

But it was more than that. I realized it had begun – though I hadn't consciously recognized it at the time – when I had stopped to look at the possum. While I had been walking I hadn't heard it, but when my own footsteps stopped a sound like other footsteps went on, just for a moment, as if someone, walking a distance behind me, had been caught off-guard by my sudden stop and had gone on a few steps before realizing I had stopped.

I kept walking. I strained to hear some betraying sound, and I thought that every now and then I did: the crunch of a twig, a clod of rough turf stubbed by an unwary toe. I desperately wanted to turn my head to look behind me, but I shouldn't let my pursuer know that I knew anyone was following me – if anyone was. Besides, I was almost certain that if there was anyone behind me, he or she was not walking on the track but moving across the orchard among the trees. Whoever it was had no need to walk on the path and run the risk of being seen if I should glance back. If it was someone who knew the area at all he would know exactly where I was going – where I *had* to go, since the track was the only route through the strip of pine forest.

I couldn't go back to the Martins' house, only three or four hundred metres behind me, because the follower was between me and the house, and if I turned back I would signal that I knew I was being followed, and if whoever followed me planned violence such a move would trigger an immediate attack. And I was too far from the house to have any real hope a scream for help would be heard.

I wanted to run. Every nerve in my being screamed at me to run.

Yet I still felt I would increase my peril if I did anything to warn that following person that I knew he was there. His enormous advantage, if he planned to attack me, was surprise. If he didn't know he had been robbed of that advantage, the scales, if not actually tipped my way, would at least be nearly balanced.

If an attack was to come, almost certainly it would be in the deep shadow of the pine forest. Until I got there – and surely I must reach it first – I must behave as if I suspected nothing. Then, the moment I reached the shadow, I would run as I had never run before. I was no champion sprinter, but I was reasonably fit and reasonably fleet of foot. And I would be running literally for my life. Desperation can lend all kinds of strength.

I must behave as if I suspected nothing. Even then I reminded myself that there might be nothing to suspect – nothing to run from. Some birds, for example, love to follow a walking human being. Motivated by sheer curiosity they will keep under cover of a hedge or undergrowth among trees and skip stealthily along until they tire of the game. Easy enough to be logical and amused by such a thing in broad daylight when one can see and know what's happening. Very different in the night when even the direction of the following sound is difficult to pinpoint.

I didn't stop to open the wire gate between the Martins'

property and Ashley Maclean's. The thought of being halted, even for the minute it would take to open and close the gate, was intolerable. I bent and slipped quickly between the second and third wires of the four-strand wire fence, and stepped almost at once into the shadow of the pines.

Since I was in the shadow I would be hidden for the moment from anyone following, and I took a second to turn and look back. Anyone following would have to come fully into the moonlight to get through the gate or the fence.

The space of open ground between the pines and the trees in the Martins' orchard was empty. I had fifty metres start, and I whirled and ran.

And as I did so I heard – almost felt – someone move in the darkness beside me.

I screamed then as I ran – blind terror behind both scream and attempt at flight. I heard the swift footsteps behind me and a man's voice I was too shocked to recognize called softly:

"Anne, wait!"

A hand closed hard over my arm before I had taken three paces and jerked me back, pulling me against him. I think I cried out again before his other hand went mufflingly over my mouth.

Then everything exploded in a confusion of violence.

Someone shouted, "Let her go!" There was the sharp thud of a fist and my assailant released me. The rustle of bushes and pine needles mixed with grunts and heavy breathing told of violent struggles, but my eyes straining in the heavy shadow could make out only dim shapes and I stood numbly, too stunned with shock to know whether I should run or stand my ground – much too stunned to have any idea what had happened.

Almost at once there were running footsteps and a powerful torch was flicked on to the scene, and Drew's voice snapped:

"What the *devil*? What's going on? Anne, are you all right?"

The combatants, standing waist-deep in undergrowth, froze as the light fell on them. Ashley Maclean had a grip on Tony's shirt-front with his left hand, his right drawn back to strike, and Tony's fists were up in an almost classic boxer's pose. For a couple of seconds they stood like figures in a photograph of a street-brawl.

Then Drew said again, sharply: "What's going *on*? Tony! Ashley!"

The two men stared at each other in the brightness from Drew's flashlight. Then Ashley let go his grip on Tony's shirt and stepped clear of the bushes and on to the path.

"Perhaps Tony would like to tell us," he said. "I'd be most interested to hear."

"Oh, I'll tell you all right!" Tony said heatedly. "A man tries to do the decent thing and gets jumped for his trouble!"

"You lay in wait for Anne and grabbed her in the shadow of the trees," Ashley said, his voice cold.

"Damn it, man, I wasn't lying in wait for her! You make it sound like a B-grade movie. I came to meet her about the time I guessed she'd be coming home. I intended to walk home with her. It just happened I met her here. She must have heard me walking – did you, Anne? – because she began to run. I didn't want her to think there was a prowler on the track so I called to her and caught hold of her. I must have given you a hell of a fright," he added apologetically to me. "When you began to scream I put my hand over your mouth to hush you till I could tell you who I was and what I was doing here. I didn't want you to rouse the neighbourhood and have the Martins bearing down on me with a double-barrelled shotgun."

He looked at me in the torchlight with the flash of a grin. "Sorry, Anne. I didn't mean to frighten you. My efforts to be a gentleman are always apt to backfire."

He turned to Ashley. "Okay, I can see why you jumped to the conclusion I was something nasty that came out of the woods. When you grabbed me and landed a punch –"

he touched his cheekbone carefully – "the same thought crossed my mind. What in the world *were* you doing here at this time of night? Or do you always take a stroll around your property at something after eleven o'clock?"

Ashley said quietly, "I had occasion to phone the Martins earlier in the evening. Evan told me Anne was there – had walked over and was intending to walk back. I felt a shade uneasy about the idea, so I decided to come along the track to keep an eye on her and make sure she got home safely."

He glanced at me very briefly and then looked away. "I didn't intend to let her know I was around. It would have taken the pleasure out of a solitary walk in the moonlight for her."

He didn't say: I knew she was afraid of me.

But he and I both knew the words.

Tony said, "Well, pedestrian traffic along this path seems to have been remarkably heavy tonight." He looked at Drew. "We need hardly ask why you're here, need we? Another escort for Anne."

"Sure," Drew said. "It didn't occur to me at first to be concerned about the idea of her walking out alone, but I got to thinking about it so I got up and dressed and came along to meet her. Anne, my love, don't go walking in the dead of night again. You start riots, and I tell you I got such a fright when you screamed and I heard the sounds of battle that it took ten years off my young life."

I had gathered enough of my wits to speak, and I tried flippancy, since anything else seemed impossible in the circumstances. "I never expected to feel I had anything in common with Helen of Troy. I'd like to think she enjoyed the war more than I did." I added, suddenly serious because in spite of myself I felt perilously close to abruptly dissolving into tears:

"I'm most terribly sorry I caused all this. Thank you all for being concerned for me. Now let's all go home. One can take only so much chivalry in one night."

Ashley and Tony shook hands and laughed at their skirmish, and Ashley said goodnight and walked off across his orchard, taking a shortcut back to his house, while Tony and Drew and I walked home via the track.

Drew chatted readily enough about all manner of things, and made it easy for us all to relax and return to normal. None of us mentioned the incident again on the walk home. I told them about seeing the possum and Tony said, "The devil was looking for ripe fruit," and Drew said they were nice creatures and didn't do much damage really, and Tony said, "Oh, Lord, don't worry. If I harmed a hair of one's head Grandma would have me deported."

By the time we reached Fairfield no one listening to us would guess we had been for anything but a pleasant, casual walk.

At the door Tony said, "Better Grandma doesn't hear of what happened tonight, don't you think?"

"Of course," Drew and I said together, and we went to our respective rooms.

Sleep didn't come to me for a long time. I had pulled the curtains back and my room was bright with moonlight, but that had nothing to do with my wakefulness. I had been filled with terror for my life, and in spite of what had happened I was far from sure my fear had been groundless.

Both Tony and Ashley had been in the pine forest when I reached it. But either of them could have been following me through the Martins' orchard and, having established the fact that I was on my way home, and knowing which way I must go, had simply dodged ahead of me through the apple trees and got to the shadow of the forest before me. If either of them had done that, he was lying when he said he simply wanted to see I reached home safely.

If Tony had followed me across the Martins' orchard, wanting to escort me home, he would have called to me then, not run ahead to wait for me in the pines.

And if it was Ashley who had followed me, concerned for my safety but feeling that if he showed himself I would be afraid, he would have continued simply to follow me, not short-cut ahead to the shadow.

Try as I would, I couldn't recall from which direction Drew had come. In fact, I simply didn't know. I had been staring at the dark confusion where only the scantiest dappling of moonlight showed where the two men were fighting. I only knew I had heard running footsteps, and then the flashlight had splintered the darkness.

I moved restlessly. What could I deduce from the way Tony had grabbed me? In the end, nothing. He may have simply wanted – very understandably – to stop my panic-stricken flight to tell me I was quite safe, and to silence me before my screams roused someone. Or he may have meant to kill me. While I lived, he could never be sure he would be heir to any part of Fairfield.

Ashley had come to my defence. But if he had lain in wait to murder me, he would have seen a perfect chance to show himself in a good light. If he defended me then, so much less chance of suspicion falling on him if, some time in the future, I met a violent end. He knew that I knew some damning evidence about him; he may well have felt he wasn't safe while I could tell the story of the bloodstained clothes, even though it was second-hand and in no way acceptable evidence in a court of law.

And Drew?

No. I would never believe that boy with the laughing eyes was a murderer. He had come to meet me because he had begun to worry about me being out alone. And yet – A seventeen-year-old worrying about someone taking a moonlit stroll? Drew had no reason to harm me. Drew had had no reason to harm Janet Chisholm. Unless he were mad. And anyone saner than Drew I found it hard to imagine. And that had been said of homicidal maniacs by wiser people than I. It was true that he had directed my suspicions against Ashley over Janet's death. He had appeared reluctant to tell me stories against Ashley, but he *had* done so, deliberately.

And if Drew and Tony and Ashley had all told the truth about their activities tonight, *who* had been following me across the Martins' orchard? Because I didn't believe any story of curious birds or animals that I had told myself to try to calm my nerves. Those had been human footsteps.

Had a fourth person walked in the moonlight with murder in his heart – or hers?

Twelve

The next days and nights did not pass easily.

Every unusual sound in the night seemed to hold menace. It took all my courage to go in broad daylight to finish cleaning the cabins for the orchard's seasonal workers, hiring of whom would begin in a couple of weeks, simply because in the cabins I was alone, isolated, vulnerable. I took to locking my door at night – a thing I had never dreamed of doing – and knew it for a useless gesture, with a window low enough for a child to climb over the sill.

I told myself that I had had a fright, but I had no real reason to suppose anyone had lied about their intentions, and in fact no-one had intended me anything but protection. But the fear lay just under the surface of my thoughts the whole time, and the strain, I knew, began to show in my face.

Mrs Maynard said to me one morning a few days after the incident, when I went into her room to collect her tray after breakfast: "Anne, are you quite well?"

I smiled – I hoped brightly. "Yes, perfectly. I haven't been sleeping well, for some ridiculousl reason. It'll pass."

"I think perhaps you should take a break, go for a holiday. Glenda could take over for a while."

I shook my head. "I couldn't very well go away now, with

the picking about to start. I'm all right. Truly."

She was looking at me keenly. "Picking won't start for a few weeks – two at least. Even a few days rest would be good for you. I'll have a word with Tony about it – and Glenda, of course." She added without giving me a chance to reply, "Sit down a minute, will you, Anne – I want to talk to you."

I sat down obediently. I suspected she was going to say something about Glenda, who to date had been simply a guest but who, when the fruit-picking began, was to go on Fairfield's payroll as seasonal labour, at least until she found out whether she liked or could handle the work.

Mrs Maynard said, "If you were in my position and owned Fairfield, how would you bequeath it?"

I stared, completely taken aback. "I couldn't possibly advise you on a business matter like that," I protested.

"I wasn't asking your advice. I asked what you would do."

I was silent a minute. Then I said slowly, "It would depend, I expect, on the way my emotions were involved."

"Then you would leave Fairfield to Tony."

"If I felt he would care for it, I expect I would."

"Don't you feel he would care for it?" she asked sharply.

I could have said: I believe he'll sell it the moment he gets the title deeds in his hands.

But in actual fact Tony had never said anything to that effect to me. "He works very hard on it," I answered.

She nodded. "Yes, he does. Which makes it seem very strange. Very honourable, certainly. It makes me very proud of him. But I didn't expect it."

I looked at her uncomprehendingly and she said, "You see, two days ago Tony came to me and asked me not to leave the bulk of my estate to him, but to make sure his cousin got an equal share."

I started, as if I'd put an unwary hand on a hot stove. It was a few moments before I managed to say, "That – that's generous of him."

My mind was racing. What – what in the *world* – was the thinking behind that move? Did he calculate that if I received a half-share in my grandmother's estate I would be prepared to accept that, accept the situation, and hold my tongue over what I knew? Did he reckon that a half-share for himself was infinitely preferable to being exposed as an imposter with no rights at all?

Or was there, somewhere under all his planning, a sense of honour, a concern that I must not be cheated? I didn't know. There was far too much of this strange man I couldn't plumb.

My astonishment must have been clear in my face, for Mrs Maynard smiled. "You find it strange that Tony should do that," she said.

"Well – he's worked here for two and a half years, and worked very hard. You told me yourself you would have been forced to leave the orchard but for him. I would have thought he might have every reason to expect that you would leave the bulk of your estate – certainly Fairfield – to him."

"You think he has the *right* to the bulk of my estate? More right than my granddaughter?"

I couldn't look at her. I had difficulty with my voice. "As I said before, I think the way a person makes a will is guided by emotional involvement, not just cold duty. Your will is a very personal thing. I could never presume to suggest what you should do."

I knew she was looking at me intently, and a sudden thought struck me with a force that made me forget for a moment who I was supposed to be. I looked at her and the words were out before I knew I was going to speak them.

"*Haven't* you bequeathed Fairfield to Tony?"

For a second I thought she would never answer such a question from her housekeeper, but her hesitation seemed to stem from the fact her thoughts were far away.

"No," she said. "A curious thing, really. I have meant to make a new will, almost ever since Tony came. But I have never changed it from the time when both my grandchildren were distant strangers. I shall, though. It is very foolish of me to procrastinate. I shall make my decision. Thank you, Anne," she added briskly. "I'm sorry to have taken up so much of your time."

I got up to take her breakfast-tray, and on impulse I bent suddenly and kissed her forehead. She looked surprised momentarily, and then smiled at me and I went out of the room rather quickly.

So, I thought, at the moment Drew Thomas is heir to Fairfield. Oh, Grandmother, I cried silently, leave it that way. But she would not, of course; how strange that she, intensely practical and businesslike person that she was, had not already changed her will in Tony's favour. What a blow to Tony if he knew.

It was the day after that incident that Tony suggested we all go down to Port Arthur for a few days' holiday before the rush of the fruit-season began.

"We could all use a few days just relaxing," he said, "and Anne hasn't yet seen our most famous tourist attraction. I know some people who have a cottage between Eaglehawk and Taranna – they use it as a weekender – and they're quite happy to have us use it. To save work for Anne and Glenda we can go to the hotel at Eaglehawk for meals. I can spare four or five days now, but once picking starts there's no chance. And Grandma's feeling well – you'd enjoy it, wouldn't you, Grandma?"

She smiled. "I would, yes. Holidays are not for me any more, but a little, leisured break like that – yes, that would be most agreeable. Drew must come also, of course."

"Of course," Tony agreed. "The cottage can hold five of us."

We set off for Port Arthur on a very warm but pleasant summer morning, four of us in Tony's own car and Drew following in his. Mrs Gootch would feed the cats and Buzz, the dog, while we were away. I felt absurdly lighthearted as we drove toward Hobart, as if for these four days I could lay aside all my problems and all my fears, and be free. In the bright morning sunshine it was easy to dismiss the memory that terror had stalked me across a moonlit orchard.

We drove through Hobart, across the bridge over the Derwent, over the causeway across Pitt Water to Sorell and down the Arthur Highway through farmland and forest, stopping occasionally to look at the scenery from some vantage-point. We walked down to the beach near Eaglehawk Neck to look at the intriguing area where the shore rocks have fractured naturally into neatly squared paving stones.

We crossed the Neck itself, where the southward-jutting Tasman Peninsula is joined to Forestier Peninsula by a strip of land little wider than the road – a factor which made the Tasman Peninsula such an effective prison site. If a convict did escape the prisons of Port Arthur, guards and dogs easily blocked his route by land to mainland Tasmania at Eaglehawk Neck, so he was forced to attempt to cross one of the bays. If he could shed his leg-irons he could attempt the long swim. If he was lucky enough or daring enough he might steal a boat. The risks were enormous and the failure rate shatteringly high. But desperate men faced with a life of futile brutality were ready to take on overwhelming odds. Some even succeeded.

We had morning tea in a little cafe, and we drove the short distance to see the Blow Hole and Tasman Arch – a natural arch of rock carved by many centuries of vicious seas crashing against the sheer rock cliffs until a less resistant area of rock eroded away, and what must have originally been a cave in the cliff has had its roof collapse, leaving the sea to thunder in through the original opening – now arched nearly ninety metres above it – and in against the solid cliffs in a cauldron of seething water. The area was still unspoiled by human habitation, a paved parking area and a safety fence the only trappings of civilization.

We all looked down at the foaming water – one moment

leaping up the walls of the cliffs inside the arch, the next draining out on the receding wave, leaving the rock floor on either side of the deepest channel under the arch exposed and gleaming wetly.

Drew said, "It must be even more spectacular by moonlight."

Mrs Maynard, standing with her hands on the safety-rail gazing at the water, said unexpectedly, "It is. Especially if there's a heavy sea running – after a storm, for instance."

She was silent a moment, a faraway look on her face. Then she added softly, "It was on a night like that, with the moon on that wild water after a storm, that my husband proposed to me. We stood just where I am standing now."

Her eyes were fixed on the water. "All those years. Yet such a *little* time."

She looked up and smiled, and her eyes were full of indestructible youth in her frail, lined face. "I am so glad we came."

We drove on to the cottage. It was of simple timber construction but practical and comfortable and quite reasonably large, with three bedrooms each equipped with two single beds, a combined kitchen and livingroom and a sunroom with a day-bed which Drew claimed as his sleeping quarters.

Mrs Maynard had a rest in her room – the main bedroom, separated from the rest of the rooms by the bathroom and a hallway. Glenda and I shared the bedroom nearest hers so that I would hear the little brass bell which was always close to her reach so that she could summon me at any time if she wanted assistance. Tony took the remaining bedroom.

Glenda offered to stay with Mrs Maynard for the afternoon while Tony and Drew and I drove the little way down to Port Arthur to see the ruins of the convict settlement. I thanked her, and we spent a fascinating hour among the remains of stone buildings whose gracious lines and symmetry of form, stones and hand-made bricks warm in the summer sun, belied the cruelty and hopelessness of the situation of the men in chains who had built them.

I walked slowly through the church whose charming architecture made it appear, at first glance among the trees, a complete structure, and only a closer look revealed there was no roof but the sky, and the windows were empty holes in a brick shell.

"I wonder what they thought about God," I said.

"Who?" asked Tony, looking slightly startled.

"The men who built this church. What did they think? Did they scoff and say there was no God, to let men live as they lived? Or did they feel that because of God, in the end no chains and no bars could cheat them of freedom?"

"I wouldn't think," Tony said drily, "they offered up too many prayers of thanksgiving. More likely while they worked here their main thought was how to smash the warder's head in."

It wasn't until we came out from the church that we realized a storm was building up rapidly – a sharp summer storm generated by the heat of the day. We hadn't long been back at the cottage when it broke, with lightning exploding in crackling flickers through the cloud and leaping to earth in flaring white lances of fire, while the thunder made the ground vibrate and the wind gusted savagely, flinging the rain against the walls and windows.

It was quickly gone, a dark wall of rain retreating to the north-east making a dramatic back-drop to a countryside suddenly bathed brilliantly in the yellow light of the setting sun, every leaf and twig and blade of grass glittering with sunlit raindrops.

I cooked a meal at the cottage stove, since Mrs Maynard would have found the effort of going out for dinner something of a trial. She went to bed early, and as I was leaving her room after making sure she was comfortable she said quietly:

"Anne."

I turned and went back to her bedside. She took my hand

and smiled up at me.

"Thank you, my dear."

I smiled. "For what?"

"For just being yourself. Oh, I have had such a happy day."

I looked down at her for a moment. "I'm glad." I bent and kissed her and she laid a hand, cool and dry, gently against my cheek.

"Goodnight, Anne."

At the door I paused with my hand on the light switch and looked back at her. She was so tiny and frail, yet the moment she came into a room she dominated it without speaking a word. She lay back against the pillows, her eyes closed, still smiling. I put the light out and went to my room, smiling to myself. She might be old and frail, but she never evoked in one the emotion of pity.

I showered and went to bed to read and luxuriate in the thought that I need not get up early in the morning. Drew was in his room listening to his transistor radio, and I could hear the television in the livingroom so I guessed Tony and Glenda were watching that.

I was more tired than I'd thought, and after perhaps an hour I put the book aside and flicked off the reading lamp.

I have no idea how long I had been asleep when Glenda shook me by the shoulder, saying my name urgently. I only know I was in that deep state of early sleep from which it is so hard to rouse, and I sat up dazedly, blinking at the light which she had switched on.

"What is it?" I asked thickly.

"Anne, I'm so afraid!" Glenda was pale, her eyes wide and frightened. "He's taken Mrs Maynard in the car to Tasman Arch."

"What?" Sleep drained out of my brain as if someone had pulled the plug in a sink of water. "Who?"

"Mrs Maynard. I was just starting my shower and he tapped on the door and said he was taking her to the Arch and if anyone asked, tell them she asked him to take her, so she could see the sea in the moonlight after a storm. But he said some very funny things tonight, and oh, Anne, I'm scared!"

I was on my feet and dressing. "*Who*?" I demanded. "Who are you talking about?"

"Tony, of course. I swear I never thought he would. Of course he wants Fairfield, but he only had to wait until she died. But he's been different lately, as if he had something on his mind. I thought – I thought it was that he'd fallen in love with you, and I –"

"She hasn't left him Fairfield," I said, frantically trying to clear my brain of sleep and the shock of what Glenda was saying. "She's never changed her will."

Glenda was staring at me, her eyes wide and dark. "He talked earlier about how easy it would be to kill someone by pushing them off a cliff, and no one could ever know it wasn't an accident. I didn't take much notice then but now I know from what he said that that's what me means to do. Oh, Anne, please stop him! Don't let Tony become a murderer!"

I pulled on a sweater and snatched up my torch. "Phone the police!" I ordered as I made for the door.

"I can't!" cried Glenda. "Not Tony!"

I spun around. "You damn well phone the police! Don't you want to stop him?'

She made a move toward the phone, fear in her eyes, and then stopped. "I can't anyway," she said dully. "The storm's put the phone out of order."

"Then go somewhere! Wake somebody and get some help!"

I dived outside and then stopped with a jolt. I had no car. I ran back into the house and thumped on Drew's door.

He was still fully dressed and had a book in his hand when he opened the door. "Anne, what's wrong?"

"I have to get to Tasman Arch, quickly!" I said.

He didn't bat an eyelid, but simply flung his book on the bed and slapped a tweed cap on his head as we ran to his car.

As he started the engine with an undisciplined roar he asked cheerfully: "Care to tell me why we're doing this?"

"Glenda thinks Tony plans to stage an accident to Mrs Maynard at the cliffs near the Arch."

"He's *what*? Oh, come on, Anne. He wouldn't kill his grandmother. Glenda's flipped!"

"She isn't his grandmother."

Drew shot a glance at me, away from the headlight-brightened road. "Pardon?"

"Mrs Maynard isn't his grandmother. He isn't Tony Maynard at all. His name's Bob Harrison. It was Tony who was killed in the accident. This man took his place. Watch the road," I added as he stared at me.

He turned his eyes back to the road, but there was a dazed look on his face and for several seconds he didn't speak. Then he let out a long, low whistle.

"How'd you find out he was a fraud? Did Glenda tell you?"

"I didn't have to find out," I said grimly. "I knew as soon as I saw him. Because Tony Maynard was my cousin."

There was another little silence before Drew said very slowly, "If I promise to keep my eyes on the road, would you mind saying that again?"

I told him as briefly as I could what I knew, and the reasons for my own masquerade.

"Hogan's ghost!" he said when I finished. "You're quite a girl, aren't you?"

"I've been quite a fool. I should have taken the chance and spoken out long ago. I think perhaps my grandmother is made of stronger stuff than I believed. I just never thought – never dreamed – he would harm her. There was no *need*!"

Somewhere in the back of my mind, behind my anguish, I recalled Glenda saying: 'Don't let Tony become a murderer!'

Even then, her foremost concern had been for the strange mixture of a man who was her brother and her hero. In Glenda's eyes I had to stop him, not primarily to save an old lady from a violent death, but to save him from tainting his hands with murder.

"The fool!" I said bitterly aloud. He's even doing it for nothing. She hasn't changed her will yet. Oh, for God's sake, Drew, can't you go faster?"

Drew was already driving like a madman, only holding the car on the road by virtue of his quick young reflexes, and normally I'd have been scared out of my wits.

He knew it, and a grin flickered over his face. "I'll remind you of that remark one day. We're almost there, Anne. But I'm sure you're wrong. Glenda's got it all wrong. Tony – Bob – whatever his name is – he wouldn't harm an old lady like Mrs Maynard. Why would he? She's old and she has a bad heart. Even if he's a greedy fraud, why would he *risk* it? He'd have to be out of his tiny mind. There's a car," he added as the headlights lit up the safety-fence at the edge of the cliff and then, apart from where they caught the salt spray flung up from the thundering sea against the cliff face, fell out into emptiness and disappeared.

He slammed on the brakes and stopped beside the other car and I was out almost before we stopped moving. But the other car was empty.

I looked both ways along the cliffs. A waning moon had risen above the storm-clouds now far out to sea, and was spreading its white light over the cliffs and the sea, but there was no one in sight, and suddenly I felt cold.

All through the wild drive here I had cherished the hope that Tony had done exactly what he had told Glenda to say he had done: driven Mrs Maynard here to see the moonlight on a storm-wild sea, as she had seen it when she promised to marry the young man who had first brought her here to see the spectacle so many years ago.

But now that hope was blown away like the spume from the wave-crests. It was unthinkable that she could have walked any distance to another vantage-point, even with Tony's help.

Drew said doubtfully beside me: "Are you sure this is Tony's car? Not just one like it? I don't recall his number."

"Yes, yes!" I said impatiently. "Anyway, that's Tony's jacket on the front seat."

The driving-side window was down and Drew reached in and took out the blue nylon padded parka. "But there are millions of coats like this!"

I took it from him and turned it around in my hands looking for something to identify it. My fingers felt a wallet in a zippered inside pocket, and I unzipped the pocket with hurried fingers, not feeling in the least that I was prying, and took the wallet out.

"It's Tony's wallet, all right," I said. "Anyway, here's his passport."

I opened the door to put the interior light of the car on, and flipped open the passport for Drew to see. Tony's photograph looked up at us, and the passport named him as Anthony Charles Maynard.

"Well, it's his, all right," Drew agreed. "The question is, where the devil is he? Where's he taken Mrs Maynard? Damn it, Anne, I still can't believe it – not Mrs Maynard! He couldn't!"

The horror of the thought seemed to have fully hit him for the first time.

But I was paying him scant attention. I was still staring at the passport, the understanding of what I was seeing crashing through my mind with the force of one of those storm-waves through Tasman Arch. And in its ebb it left a sickened certainty that the need for urgent action was over.

We were too late.

I gripped the edge of the car door for support. "He couldn't!" Drew said again.

"Couldn't he?" I said grimly. "Couldn't he?" I held out the passport. "Drew, *look* at it! What is it?"

He blinked. "It's a passport – Tony's passport, of course.

Come *on*, Anne, we've got to find them!"

I shook my head. "It's too late. Whatever he's planned, he's done by now."

I dropped passport and wallet on the front seat with the jacket and we started toward the cliff top.

"Drew," I said urgently, "think! Think! It's a passport – a British passport issued before he left England. It's in the name of Anthony Charles Maynard. *But it has Bob Harrison's photograph on it!*"

Drew stopped in his tracks and looked at me. "Oh, Lord, yes! Yes, I see. Of course. It's a phony passport. But –" he stopped.

I nodded. "That means *he knew* before he left England that he was going to take Tony's place."

Drew was motionless, his slender boy's form frozen in shock. "But that would mean – that would mean he knew the real Tony Maynard was going to die!"

"Exactly. It means cold, calculated, long-planned murder." I shivered. "Drew, I don't think we're going to find Mrs Maynard alive."

"Well," he said, and there was fury in his voice, "we're damned well going to try! If he's harmed her, I'll kill him."

Something in the quiet way he spoke the last sentence was chilling. The boy who had driven here with breakneck recklessness on an errand he hadn't fully understood, had had his youth snatched away, and in the boy's place stood a man, filled with the ancient savagery that can rise up in defence of what one loves. For he had loved my grandmother with that affinity of spirit which can exist between the aged and the very young.

"Go that way along the cliff," he ordered crisply, pointing. "I'll go the other way. If you see him, for the love of Heaven, bluff – don't let him guess you know what he's about."

And he was gone.

I started to walk slowly along the cliff, watching the white rage of water against the night-blackened rocks, picking my way carefully, since a stumble was something I could not afford, and live. One thought kept nagging at me even through the ache of grief for my grandmother and the burn of bitter anger against the evil of the man she had trusted: where was Tony?

If he wanted to commit a murder which looked like an accident there was no need to go any farther than the spot where his car was parked. Afterwards he could say Grandmother had been determined to leave the safety-fenced area and walk farther along the cliff, and while his attention was distracted for a moment, she had overbalanced, and fallen.

"Is that you, Anne?" His voice held a note of surprise, but no more than that.

I spun around. He was standing near the safety-fence, between me and the cars, and for the first time I realized my vulnerability and I knew why Drew had told me not to let Tony guess I knew why he was here.

Somehow I managed to make myself walk back toward him. Somehow I made myself say: "I *thought* it was your car. It was worth coming to see, wasn't it? That rough sea is quite a sight in the moonlight."

"Yes," he said. "Quite."

He was standing still, waiting for me to get back to him, and I was almost beside him before I realized I was walking straight into a trap. If he had planned to try to convince me that my grandmother had met with an accidental death, he would have pretended agitation, would have hurried to meet me with distressed-sounding explanations. But he was simply standing motionless, waiting.

I stopped, staring at him, knowing it was too late to run. Perhaps it had always been too late, from that first day I had seen him in the store.

"What is it?" I heard myself say, and my voice was pitched too high.

He simply stood there, looking at me, his face expressionless in the moonlight.

"What have you done with my grandmother?" I demanded. The time for bluffing was over. "Where is she?"

"Fast asleep in bed, I expect," he said.

And somehow I knew he meant it.

"But Glenda said –" I stopped, knowing as surely as if he had drawn a knife exactly why I was here: I was here because he wanted me here, and he had known that the thought of danger to Grandmother would bring me.

He laughed. "Oh, yes. Good old Glenda. Entirely predictable, entirely reliable."

"I don't think even Glenda will let you get away with murder."

"She had better." His tone was quite casual, and it made me feel ill.

I said bitterly, "You fool! You didn't have to kill me. I'd decided to quietly disappear and let you have Fairfield, since Grandmother wanted you to have it."

"Really?" His face in the moonlight was incredulous. "You honestly thought I'd take a chance on that?"

"Curiously enough," I said slowly, "yes. It never occurred to me that you might kill me. Naive of me, wasn't it?"

I was keeping my eyes on him, but my aching attention was on the bush near the cliff-top on the other side of the parking area behind him. He couldn't have guessed that Drew had come with me. Just how much chance Drew would have of overpowering him I didn't know, but, with the element of surprise thrown in, two of us stood some kind of chance against him, unless he was armed. I must keep him talking, and pray that Drew would come back soon, having given up his search along the cliffs, and size up the situation before Tony knew he was there. Whether I lived or died depended now on Drew.

Tony – curious, I still thought of him by that name – was saying: "My dear girl, you mean you honestly thought I would risk a fortune to your good nature? After all I've done to set myself up?"

"I didn't know until tonight that you were a murderer already."

He raised his eyebrows. "Janet? Now how the devil did you find that out? The prying little bitch deserved it. I was foolish enough to keep my own passport in my room, in a locked drawer where I thought it would be safe. I didn't know about Janet's charming habit of poking about in the hope that she might pick up something to serve as a basis for blackmail. A locked drawer, far from discouraging her, inspired her to pick the lock – a handy little trick she'd picked up in the course of her private-nursing career. She worked on the principle that whatever people want to keep private may yield a nasty secret to hold over them. When she found a passport in the name of Robert William Harrison who was supposed to have died in a motor accident, bearing the photograph of someone who called himself Anthony Maynard, she knew she was on to a good thing. She'd never have let up. She'd have clung on to me like a leech, and she'd have bled me white. I wasn't going to put up with that."

I was only half hearing him. Above my own freezing fear of him a joyous realization was surging, a running warmth of life through my veins.

"Janet?" I said stupidly. "Janet Chisholm? You killed *Janet*?"

His eyes narrowed. "Who did you think?"

I misunderstood his meaning. "I thought – Ashley had killed her."

"Everyone thought Ashley had killed her," Tony said impatiently. "I knew he'd be suspect number one, so I pinched some of his clothes to wear. Then if anybody's clothes had blood on them they'd be his, not mine. And Ashley Maclean had the motive of unrequited passion – at least in some people's eyes, though I've always wondered if there might not have been something else – while Tony Maynard had no motive at all. I put the clothes back at his place, but as they didn't arrest him, I gather he found them first and was able to get rid of them."

"You tried to frame Ashley for murder!"

He shrugged. "I didn't much mind whether they pinned it on him or not. It was just a precaution to make sure no heat was turned on me."

He took one step toward me and stopped. "You were surprised when I said I'd killed Janet Chisholm. Yet you thought I was a murderer. Who did you think I'd killed?"

I had nothing to lose by telling him, and I might have everything to gain by playing for time. Surely Drew wouldn't extend his search of the cliffs far. He must be back soon. And while I had certainly never wanted to die, now I had everything on earth to live for.

Ashley was not a murderer, and I was in love with him. I hadn't even admitted it to myself before, because it hurt too much.

"You killed Tony Maynard," I said.

He didn't move, but I could sense shock hit him.

"How in hell," he said very softly, "do you know that?"

"Tonight when – when I came here." To my horror I had almost said: When we came here.

"I wanted to be quite sure it was your car. There was a jacket on the front seat. I picked it up to see if I could identify it, and I felt your wallet in the pocket, and I opened it and it had your passport in it. Only it's not your passport. It's a fraud, like you. And that meant you knew before you left England that you were going to take over Tony's role. You must have planned for months to kill him."

There was a silence that seemed to stretch on forever.

"Well, well. What a clever little girl you are," he said.

He laughed. "When Tony found out what the old lady was being offered for the orchard, he suggested we come out and he'd become the blue-eyed boy and inherit, and we'd share the loot in the fullness of time. He needed me because he was bone lazy. On his own he'd never have been able to impress his grandmother enough to induce her to leave her precious Fairfield to him. But I could see I was going to do all the work while he did all the charming, and in the end I'd have to depend on his generosity for compensation. Tony being Tony, that was no guarantee, I assure you."

There was no movement behind him, no sign of Drew.

"So you staged the accident," I said. "Did you believe you could get away with it?"

"I did, and I do. Why not? Here I am in possession of Tony Maynard's birth certificate and passport. I fit his general description. No one who knew him – or me – is ever likely to come out here – except Glenda, and she'd never give me away."

"Does she know you killed Tony?"

"No. And she won't know I killed you, either. I'll tell her when I went to get Mrs Maynard the old lady was asleep, so I didn't disturb her, but decided to come down here on my own anyway. I didn't see you. You must have been poking along the cliffs in the moonlight and missed your footing. Glenda will believe that because she'll want to believe it."

He shrugged. "There was no need for her to know about Tony. I killed him with one hit with a wheel-brace, by the way. He never knew what happened. Then I drove the car toward the edge of the road – it was a bit hard to find a good spot with no safety-fence – and jumped out at the last minute as it went over. It had to be carefully judged, and I damn near went with it as it was."

His eyes gleamed with the remembered excitement of the danger.

"I climbed down the cliff to the wreck – I'd kept a torch in my pocket so I could see what I was doing – and set it alight. Fortunately the petrol tank had ruptured and there was petrol everywhere, so all I had to do was light a match. There was more petrol about than I'd realized, and the fire flared back on me – that's how I got my hands a bit burned, and my clothes and hair were singed and my eyebrows burnt off, but in the end it worked out very well, because it gave my story positive confirmation. I got a hell of a fright, actually, but I put out the fire on my clothes quickly, and I even remembered to chuck the torch into the fire.

"But I knew that even aside from the burns, which were relatively minor after all, I had to injure myself to make it all look real. It's a very hard thing to do – deliberately hurt yourself. Especially as my hands were hurting and my face felt raw. I climbed part-way up the cliff, and then let myself fall. My injuries were quite genuine, I assure you. I was a very sick boy for a while. But it established my credentials absolutely."

"Congratulations," I said bitterly.

Where was Drew?

Tony made a slight bow. "Thank you. So you see that after all that, I wasn't likely to let anyone stand in my way, was I?"

"And so you did a second murder, and now you intend a third. Do you realize how the risks are multiplying?"

"I've never minded risks."

"And how," I demanded, "are you going to explain the fact that I was Anne Beaconsfield and kept my identity secret? My real identity will be found out. You can't prevent that. How come you didn't recognize your own cousin?"

"Ah, but my story will be that I did, of course. But I took my cue from you. You had this idea that you wanted your grandmother to like you for *yourself*, before you told her who you were. It was your wish, and I went along with it, no matter that I thought it somewhat a foolish whim."

He hesitated and then said: "I'm sorry you turned out to be who you are. I cared about you. We'd have made a good team."

I stared at him, and suddenly I realized: He's finding it hard, I thought; that's why he keeps talking; for the first time, he's finding it hard to kill in cold blood; he wants me to run, to do something to trigger the need for action.

Tony was at his best when there was urgent need for action. He revelled in it.

He said quite casually, "Oh, by the way, there's no point in hopefully scanning the countryside behind me for your young friend. He isn't coming to do the daring rescue bit."

I felt as if a freezing drift of air had settled over me. "What do you mean?"

"I watched you arrive, from the cover of the bushes. I expected you both. I knew I'd better deal with Drew first, so I followed him. I expect the authorities will assume one of you somehow fell, and the other, attempting rescue, was also swept away. I, of course, will be profoundly distressed, because I must have just missed meeting you here."

"You killed him!" Grief and rage rose through my whole being in a fire that swept away the chill. "You killed that boy!"

There were loose stones on the ground here near the cliff edge. I bent and snatched one up and leapt at Tony, reason swamped by hatred, filled with only one desire: to smash that piece of rock into his confident, smiling face.

Had he been taken by surprise I might have succeeded, but I realized in a moment that he had told me about Drew in a deliberate move to trigger me into the action he so needed to make it easier for him to kill me.

He was ready, and he flung up one arm to parry the blow, and grabbed me with his other hand.

Even so the rock struck a glancing blow along his cheek and as he jerked his head back his grip on me loosened. The stone flew from my hand, and I whirled and ran.

He shouted a curse, and then thudding heart and gasping breath as I ran swamped out every other sound, just as terror and desperate concentration on keeping my footing swamped out every other thought.

In my high-school days I had been a fair sprinter, but that was ten years before, and the rock-and-bush-strewn cliff-top bore no resemblance to a running-track. In moments I realized I would never out-run a man as fit as Tony. I had to employ some other tactic.

Stunted coastal shrub grew fairly thickly near the cliff

edge, and without slackening speed I whirled aside and plunged into it, a thousand twigs and small branches clutching and clawing at me. Several times I stumbled over stones or cracked my shins against larger rocks. Once I tripped and fell sprawling headlong.

My face hit hard earth with bruising force and I lay half stunned, my skin crawling with horror as I waited for Tony's crashing footsteps to stop beside me, his hands to close on me and drag me back toward the hungry sea.

I don't know how many seconds it took for me to realize it wasn't going to happen. There were no pursuing footsteps, no sounds of someone crashing through the bush after me. The very fall that had seemed the ultimate disaster had in fact saved me. He would have been following the sounds of my fear-winged flight, and with the abrupt cessation of those sounds he had lost me.

I sat up very slowly. I was far enough from the sea now to hear sounds of bushes being thrust aside, twigs snapping, in what would be a search as desperate as my flight had been. Because Tony knew that his liberty for the rest of his life depended as much on finding me as my survival depended on eluding him.

There was no sound but the sea.

Was he standing motionless in some shadow a few metres away, straining to hear me begin to move again?

I waited till my breathing steadied and I could begin to think again. I tried to close my mind against the rage and grief at the thought of what Tony had done to Drew – tried to shut it out because it was a blinding pain, and if this murderer was not to be allowed to get away with all the evil he had done, I would need every shred of alertness I possessed, in order to have a chance to live to accuse him.

I must try to get back to the cars. I knew Drew had left his keys in the ignition.

Almost as soon as the thought occurred to me, I realized how stupid I was. That was exactly what Tony would expect me to do.

I must find my way out on to the road, avoiding the parking area by the Arch, and go for help. I couldn't remember just where the nearest habitation was, but it wasn't far away. And, I realized with some surprise, it was still relatively early in the night: a car just might come along the road – a courting couple, perhaps, on their way to the parking-lot I must avoid – and I could flag it down.

Very cautiously, I began to move in a roughly westerly direction, away from the sea, which would bring me fairly quickly to the road. Once I reached the road I couldn't have more than a couple of kilometres to go to reach the village, and there must be houses along the way.

Parting bushes carefully, moving as quietly as possible, I gained confidence with every step, because there were no sounds of pursuit. Tony, beyond doubt, had done the only thing he could do once he had lost me: he had gone to set a trap. He had gone back to the parking area to lie in wait for me. He would realize, presently, that I was not coming, and he would then begin to search for me. He would almost certainly guess what I had done, and would set out to find me. But I would hear a car well before the lights fell on me, and any car coming from the direction of the Arch I could avoid by taking to the bush until it had passed.

As I emerged into the open, with the road before me, I looked both ways and stood for a moment listening. I could still hear the thunder of the surf, and my own breathing was rough with tension and exertion, but that was all.

I stepped out on to the road and turned in the direction of Eaglehawk Neck, fighting a desire to run in blind panic. I must not. If I ran, the pounding of my footsteps and my heart would lessen the chances of hearing a car approaching, and the one thing I could be very sure of was that Tony had not given up the search for me.

I made myself keep to a fast walk. I think at every step I expected him to leap out of the bush beside me, and my stomach nerves were so knotted they hurt, but I made myself not run.

I don't know how far I'd gone when I heard the car. I seemed to have been walking for hours, though in reality I suppose I hadn't gone more than half a kilometre. I scuttled off the road like a scared rabbit before I realized with a joyful leap of my heart that it was coming the other way – from Eaglehawk Neck. It was the one thing I hadn't really dared to hope for: a chance visitor to the Tasman Arch by night, or possibly someone who had a cottage back in the trees returning home.

I was safe.

I leapt out into the middle of the road waving my arms frantically. The driver jammed on his brakes and as I ran to the driving-side window he began to open the door in evident concern.

"Please!" I gasped. "Please help me! I must get the police."

"Of course," he said, and his hand clamped over my wrist as the door opened wide enough to put on the interior light and I stared into Tony's smiling face.

He had a knife in his other hand, held with deadly purpose, but I doubt if he really needed it. The sheer shock, on top of all the other things which had happened in the previous hour or so, drained me in an instant of all strength, all ability to go on fighting. Once when I was surfing a sudden large wave had picked me up and dumped me viciously down on the sand, knocking the breath agonizingly from my lungs and rendering me for a few dreadful moments utterly helpless.

That was exactly the way I felt as Tony dragged me into the car, sliding over into the passenger seat as he did so.

"You drive," he said pleasantly. "And do exactly what I tell your or you'll die a much nastier death than falling over a cliff, I assure you." He held the knife close against my body.

I obeyed. I was swamped by a weariness beyond description. I didn't ask where we were going, because I knew. We were going back to the cliff top. It had all been for nothing.

"I guessed what you'd do," Tony said jauntily. "There wasn't much else you *could* do, really, except try to get to habitation. It would be too risky for you to go back for the car – though just to make sure I took the keys out of Drew's car. So once you took to the bush I didn't try to follow you, because it'd be too easy to lose you. I went straight back and drove up along the road so that when I came back you'd think I was a stranger. Oh, it was all chancy, of course, and I cursed myself for letting you get away, but it all turned out all right."

I drove like a robot, numb, not able to think; totally defeated.

I stopped the car where he told me and he followed me out, one hand gripped around my wrist, the other holding the knife-point against my back. In a like manner we climbed the safety-fence by the cliff edge. I hadn't spoken since I had seen his face in the car. I had nothing left to say.

He talked all the time – brightly, happily, immensely pleased with himself. He told me he had tried to kill Drew by loosening the wheel-nuts on the tractor. "Very hit-or-miss, awfully amateurish I'm afraid, but the chance was there and worth a try. The old lady was too fond of him for my liking. I always had an uneasy feeling she might decide to leave him a good share of her estate. I'd have felt much more secure without him."

I don't remember the rest of what he said.

I was aware only of the edge of the cliff, of the waves in the moonlight leaping up the wet black rocks as if eager to snatch me away. But shock, despair, weariness – something – had dulled even that.

I remember Tony peered over the side and said: "This will do."

Ashley's voice from a little distance snapped: "Maynard! Let her go!"

Tony and I jerked our heads around together.

Ashley was standing perhaps thirty or forty paces away. I

could see he had something in his hand and for one wild moment of hope I thought he had a pistol. Then in dismay I saw it was only a stone he had snatched up.

For an instant we all stood like exhibits in a waxworks.

Then Tony laughed and wrenched me toward the edge of the drop. I came alive and screamed in warning: "Ashley! He has a knife!"

I dropped on my knees to try to find a grip on a rock, a shrub, anything to give me a purchase to try to resist the strength of Tony's arm that was forcing me over the edge. But my groping fingers found nothing to hold, and Tony's strength was far too much for me. I felt the spray from the bursting surf swept up the cliff on to my face.

And Tony's fingers suddenly released their hold on me. It took me perhaps a second to realize it, and I looked up at him.

He was staggering, slumping to his knees. Limply and without a sound he fell from the cliff on to the rocks far below.

I heard Ashley's running footsteps, and in a moment his arms were around me. Even before he could draw me back from the cliff we saw the waves break over where Tony's body lay, and when they surged out again the rock was bare.

I turned my head to bury my face against Ashley's shoulder, and I could taste the salt from the sea on my lips. I will remember that as long as I live.

Ashley said nothing. His arms were wrapped around me and he held me crushed against him.

Then a voice said with a gallant attempt at casual cheerfulness: "You mean this romance has been going on right under my nose? Remember, Anne, I *told* you Ashley was a crack bowler and the best fieldsman I ever saw? I was only a little kid when I saw him throw down a fellow's wickets, side on, from forty metres out in a State match, but I've never seen anything as good as what he did tonight. A hunk of rock, in the moonlight, and he can hit a bloke's head at thirty paces! Hogan's ghost!"

My fingers gripped on Ashley's sweater, I very slowly raised my head, sure I must be mad, or at best hallucinating.

"Drew?" I said wonderingly. "Drew?"

"The very same. Who else?"

I turned and stared at him. There was dried blood on his face, and he was holding his cap in his hand, and even in the moonlight I could see he was unsteady on his feet.

"But he said he'd killed you!" I sprang to him and hugged him and illogically burst into tears.

"Hey, old thing, it's all right!" he assured me. "Steady there. Oh, I guess he thought he'd killed me, all right. But what he didn't know was that Mum always used to worry so because I rode my bicycle through traffic to school and I reckoned I'd look a proper ninny in a safety helmet when nobody else wore one, so I got a fibreglass reinforcement put in this cap to keep Mum happy. Reckon it saved my life tonight. Lord knows how long I was out cold. As it is I feel as if Mt. Wellington fell on me. Sorry, Anne. Not exactly the knight in shining armour, was I? I just staggered here to see the final act."

Then in a changed, shaken voice, he said, "What happened, Anne? What happened to Mrs Maynard? Were we – just too late?" His eyes were dark with the pain of that thought.

"No, Drew," I said gently. "She was never here. He knew if he threw out a few hints to Glenda she'd panic and tell me exactly what she did. But the plan was to bring me here. It was my death he wanted, not Mrs Maynard's. He knows she can't live long. But I was different, because I knew who he was. I could ruin everything. Odd. I was such a fool. It never occurred to me that he might try to harm me. But then, of course, I didn't know he was already a killer."

Ashley was looking fixedly at me. "It seems to me there is

a very great deal more I don't know."

"That's another thing," Drew said. "Ashley, where in Heaven's name *did* you come from?"

I put my hand in Ashley's and felt his fingers grip mine comfortingly. He said, "Later. First, we have to find a phone and call the police."

I shivered. "No one can do anything, can they? I mean, that fall – he would have been dead before the sea took him. No rescue –"

"No." Ashley's face was grim. "But a man is dead, and we have to report it."

It seemed an eternity later that we all sat in the kitchen of the holiday house Tony had rented.

The police sergeant who had come to the cliffs with two constables, ropes and powerful torches and followed by an ambulance with two more men, must have been somewhat curious, to say the least, over Ashley's bald statement that Tony had been trying to kill me when he – Ashley – had hit him and he had overbalanced and fallen; but he gave no indication of it, merely asking Drew and me if that was correct. He looked at my bruised cheek and the dried blood on Drew's face oddly and said laconically to Ashley: "You'd better get those two home. The homicide people will doubtless be along to see you tomorrow – maybe even tonight – to get statements and so on. And maybe he –" jerking his head at Drew – "needs a doctor."

We sat drinking tea. Glenda sat alone by the window, pale, shocked, silent, drained of vitality.

Ashley, I knew now, had driven down to the area that evening in search of us. He had just found out from Harry Gootch at Fairfield where we had gone.

"I was worried," he had told us while we waited at the cliff for the police. "And I'd done an awful lot of thinking since you told me I'd been seen the morning after Janet Chisholm's death, with a bundle of bloodstained clothes."

Drew started.

"I reckoned the only person who would know about those clothes would be the person who pushed them behind the hot-water system in the laundry, and he wouldn't have to see me with them at all, because he'd know I must have found them before the police arrived, or surely I'd have been arrested. It was only the purest chance I did find them, I might add. And from there I calculated that the only person who would have told you was Tony. Which by my reasoning made Tony the murderer, and not a very safe person for you to be with. When I knew he'd brought you all down here I felt he was up to something, and I was afraid – horribly afraid. I had no idea why he'd want to harm you, or what might happen, though in retrospect it seemed he may have tried to kill you that night when you were walking home from the Martins' place. I only knew I had to be here, to try to keep some sort of guard over you at least until I could try to warn you."

"It wasn't Tony who told Anne about the clothes," Drew said flatly. "I did. It gave me a hell of a fright when I saw you stuffing them into the incinerator. Sorry. I mean, I'm glad – awfully glad – it wasn't what I thought."

Ashley smiled faintly. "Thanks. I got a hell of a fright, too, when I found them. I'd no idea then what had happened, but I didn't have to be a genius to guess I was being set up for something very ugly. Had I been noble enough, I guess I'd have taken the clothes straight to the police, but I was too big a coward and my only thought was that I had no witness as to where I'd been the night before, and so I just wanted to get rid of those clothes as fast as possible."

"I was scared," Drew said, "because – well, I was at Oakhill one day and I overheard Janet trying to blackmail you over – over your father and brother, all those years ago. I knew she had to be lying about that, but when I knew she was dead –" He stopped.

Ashley nodded. "Dear Heaven. That too."

Drew said unhappily , "Sounds as if I spend all my spare

time spying on you."

Ashley said slowly, "Funny, I'd always thought of Janet as a friend, till that day." He paused, and then went on, "I asked her why she'd waited so long to play her rotten games. She said she'd never thought of it till she came to Fairfield and saw me again. I challenged her to tell me exactly what she had seen. She laughed in my face and said she hadn't seen me at all that day, but no-one was to know that. She'd been there at the time all right – I checked on that. She said all she had to do was to spread the rumour and my life would become hell. I told her that if I ever heard any such rumour had started, I'd kill her. I think she believed I meant it. Perhaps I did."

When Ashley had found out from Harry Gootch where we were staying, he had driven down to the cottage. Puzzled by the fact the cars were missing, he had gone to the door and knocked, and made Glenda tell him where we had gone. He could see she was scared, though she wouldn't tell him any details. He had parked his car in the bushes, out of sight, and come the rest of the way to the cliffs on foot so that he could assess the situation without being seen.

"I was so nearly too late," he said, his arm around me. "When I saw him with you on the cliff – I would have traded my life for a rifle. All I had was my one and only skill – and that was rusty. I'd never prayed so hard as when I prayed I'd hit him." He paused, and looked to the far distant dark line of storm-cloud, still back-lit with lightning.

"Strange, to pray to kill a man."

I touched his cheek. "You didn't know he would fall."

His eyes glinted, hard as glass. "I didn't care, either."

Ashley and Drew and I had talked a great deal while we waited at the cliffs for the police, and once Drew had tactfully gone off to look at his car to see whether he could start it without the key, because Tony had taken it. He had left us alone, and Ashley had said to me things which belong only to us.

Now, sitting in the kitchen, we were all strangely silent. Perhaps partly because we had felt so much emotion in so short a time. Perhaps because of the stunned, bereft figure of Glenda by the window.

The telephone was functioning again after the storm and Ashley had called a local doctor and asked him to come to see Drew. Drew had violently objected that there was nothing wrong with him, but Ashley and I both felt he must surely have some degree of concussion, and Ashley point-blank refused to leave me in order to take Drew to the doctor.

"You've had more than enough for one night," he told me. "I'm not leaving you."

I stood up. "I must go and see to Mrs Maynard," I said. "She may have been wakened by all the coming and going."

"If she is awake," Ashley said quietly, "what are you going to tell her?"

I paused, feeling a dreadful hollowness in the pit of my stomach. "Nothing tonight," I said. "Not even that he's dead, let alone who he was. It can wait. I want a doctor to be here when I tell her in the morning. But the morning is soon enough."

I shook my head. "I wish she didn't have to know. But she does."

Drew said, looking at me with a bewildered expression: "Anne, did you really mean it when you said you planned to leave? Just walk away and never tell anyone who you were and let Tony *have* Fairfield?"

"Yes."

"But – why? He had no right to it!"

"No," I said tiredly. "But I had no idea then that he was a murderer. I thought he was just an adventurer who saw an opportunity, and chanced his arm."

"He still had no right to it!"

I smiled faintly. "Didn't he? That's what it took me so

long to decide. Drew, Fairfield is Mrs Maynard's, to do with as she chooses. He had worked, worked fiercely hard, on Fairfield. He was never anything but courteous and thoughtful and kind to my grandmother. He was just what she needed most: someone to love. For some curious reason she never quite trusted him enough to change her will and leave him Fairfield outright, but she loved him. Lord knows, *I'd* never been any help to her. Until he came, you were the only person she had to love. *And* she trusted you."

Drew flushed with pleased embarrassment.

I went along the passageway to Grandmother's room. It would be a great pity, I thought suddenly, if she ever changed her will. Drew should be the one to own Fairfield, not I. He was the only person who loved it as Margaret Maynard had loved it. And I – I reflected with a joyful smile as the thought surfaced dazzlingly in this night of nightmares – I would have Ashley, and that was more than enough.

I dreaded the morning, when Grandmother had to learn the truth, but as I slipped silently into her room my heart was full of hope and something close to confidence.

I need not have been afraid that we had disturbed her. She lay sleeping just as I had left her, one frail hand on the pillow beside her face, her lips still in a faint smile at the happiness of the day and the memories it had brought her.

I stood looking down at her, as the moonlight lay across her bed, for several seconds before I understood. But even before I reached for her cold wrist I knew that I was alone in the room.